FIRESTORM

By Jessica Schluff

Copy write 2016

All writes reserved

To all of the people that I love, you are the inspiration for my characters.

Thank-you so much

PART ONE-KABOOM

Chapter 1

The mall on the ground floor of the Carlton Tower was packed with a large post-Christmas and pre-New Years crowd taking advantage of the year-end clearance deals during their holiday time off. Eric Bell had planned for today to be *the day* because he knew that the stores would be the perfect combination of short staffed and overrun by customers because of the holiday season. He knew that the hectic atmosphere would make it easier for him and four of his five associates to move through the mall and complete their mission with deadly efficiently.

Eric was the perfect man for jobs such as this because he actually put effort in to looking average. He was thirty years old, had brown hair and blue eyes, was slightly above average height, and was a healthy weight for a man his age. He also had a healthy Caucasian skin tone.

The grooming job he did on his hair and face was largely dependent on what identity he had to portray. For this job, he kept his hair long enough to run his fingers through to style, but short and neat enough to fit with his cleanly shaven face.

For this operation, Eric and the others on his team had been hired by a man that they knew by reputation only. Amilio Scarleto's reputation said he was not someone who takes no for an answer, but unlike the others on his team, Eric didn't need to be intimidated because he appreciated the challenge that came with serving such a criminal kingpin. Eric was so intrigued, in fact, that he initially refused payment and agreed to follow Scarleto's step-by-step instructions instead of his own plan without argument; but that was then and this was now and now, he was regretting that decision.

As instructed, Eric consistently and inconspicuously swiped items from overrun shops that he knew would not notice that the items had disappeared until long after he'd gone. He then intermittently exchanged the items he wore for the ones that he'd stolen. When Eric had entered the mall, he was wearing a long-sleeved grey shirt and black jeans, but by the time he reached the elevators at the mall's center he was wearing a black T-shirt, dark wash blue jeans, a black baseball cap, and sunglasses. He had also changed his outfit drastically a few times before reaching the elevators; the only pieces of his attire that he consistently kept with him were a plain black backpack and some shopping bags.

The shopping bags held a handful of items he had legitimately bought just for the bags that came with them because they helped him blend in with the other shoppers and kept his hands free while carrying certain items.

The stealing and the changing in and out of stolen items he was intended to make him harder to follow on security footage, but Eric knew that once he was done, the security footage would be unusable. Eric found this step unnecessary, but Scarleto was too frightened of technology to understand why.

Eric felt that the thievery was more likely to get him caught and end the mission than any surveillance would because the constant changing of clothes created the risk of other people noticing that he was not-so-average and the thefts could potentially leave him at the mercy of mall security. In his mind, that was just one of many flaws in the plan he was forced to follow.

Because he was focussing on his dissatisfaction with his assignment, Eric ran into a hustling couple. They called him out on his lack of tact, drawing lots of unwanted attention to him. Eric recognized his irritation was taking away from the success of the mission, so he breathed a steadying sigh of relief when he reached the elevator and began to move into the other phases of the plan.

At the elevator, he hovered at the garbage can aligned below the elevator buttons and opened one of his shopping bags. The bag held the cheap wallet that he had stuffed with all of his ID and credit cards that he had made for this job. The shopping bag also held a bottle of potent acid he brought from home. He took out the bottle, threw away the loaded wallet, and all of the shopping bags carrying the other stolen items he was no longer utilizing. He uncapped the bottle and salted the interior of the garbage can with the acid before throwing the bottle in too. He then pressed the button and boarded the elevator. As the doors closed behind him, he broke into a smile which expanded into a laugh. He watched the hoards of selfish people hustle, bustle, and barter for useless trinkets and hollow gifts. They had no idea that in a few minutes many of them would die, others would be injured, and all of them would be party to the latest historic terrorist event. He had all the power now and better still, all of the evidence of his identity and his involvement were currently dissolving away in the acid filled garbage can.

No one noticed him laughing as the doors closed, so they missed their last chance to stop him.

Once the doors closed, his laughter immediately ceased because he knew he had to focus and work quickly. He swung his backpack from his shoulder to the elevator floor and pulled an old fashioned, black, hard-shell briefcase and a grey business suit from the backpack. He carefully changed into the suit as the elevator climbed. He put the clothes he changed out of into the backpack then rolled the backpack up and locked it the briefcase which currently contained a sophisticated and powerful bomb that only consumed less than half the briefcase. He successfully completed his transformation by the sixth floor and watched as the numbers rose from six, to seven, and then to eight.

With the rise to the eighth floor, Eric's nerves and irritation returned. His first team member was scheduled to meet him in the elevator at the seventh floor and did not. Eric found some relief however, as at the ninth floor, the second team member was expected to join them and the doors opened. For a brief moment, Eric's faith in the plan increased, but it faded again as the elevator was boarded.

A soft and kind looking mother wearing a fuzzy red jacket and a practical, warm-looking, purple scarf got on. She was a pale-skinned brunet. The sight of her and her occupied baby stroller effectively crushed his hopes. He remembered that there were medical offices on a few of the floors above them and he initially concluded that it was more likely that she was taking her baby in for an appointment than she was a terrorist.

As the doors began to close behind her; a forty-something, athletic looking, and business-like Asian man ran up breathlessly shouting, "Hold that door PLEASE!" and the woman reopened the door at the last possible second.

When he entered the elevator, he thanked the woman and then turned his back to her and Eric. He took out a fat flip phone, pressed some buttons, and said into the phone, "Yes, hello, I'm looking for E.B. Dell..." Eric recognized those words as the code he'd made to help him identify his first team member; the one that should've been on the elevator already.

According to the plan, the first team member who was late knew the other team members well. The code that the Asian man just offered up was intended to allow Eric to identify him and he would then vouch for the other members. Eric took a half step towards him, intending to ask him why the plan was slowly falling apart, but before his approach could be noticed the woman surprised both men by pulling a gun out from under her baby and pointed it at the Asian man. Both men were shocked and nervously raised their hands. "You were supposed to be here before me; what kept you?" The woman asked calmly.

"I had a f-flat tire," the Asian man stammered. He opened his suit jacket slightly revealing a smudged stain on the shirt beneath it. The stain looked as though the man had grease on his hand from a tire change and attempted to scratch an itch spreading the grease effectively across the shirt. The opening of his jacket also drew their attention to his pants which were also consistently scuffed. "The tire obviously slowed down my getting here, but then I felt I had to do what I could to clean up so I would draw less attention. Time got even further away from me while I was cleaning, so I had to take the stairs to catch up to the schedule. Sorry. Shouldn't you also be worried about the cameras?" The Asian man looked up in the corner past the women's head where the elevator camera was according to the specifics the team was given.

    Eric knew what the man was thinking and picked up the conversation, "The camera's on a feedback loop, but you should probably put the gun away anyway in case someone who's not a part of this team wants to take a ride and ends up being spooked instead." The woman abruptly turned her focus and her gun on Eric, but he knew that he had taken her by surprise and kept the upper hand. "C'mon, I know you were expecting two of us. I made the plan." To verify his bold statement, he answered the Asian man's code. "Funny you should call me, when I'm right here."

The woman looked at the Asian man. He confirmed the code and she relaxed the gun slightly, but she continued to study Eric suspiciously. Eric ignored her and turned his attention to the Asian man saying, "Unexpected delays or not, you still should've met me on the sixth floor."

The Asian man pulled a gun out from his belt and pointed it at Eric, explaining, "It was the seventh floor." The woman, once again surprised, reaffirmed her killer focus on Eric.

"I know that, I was testing you. This plan is falling apart quickly; I needed to make sure you are prepared to act when the time comes. Also, car trouble is an easy thing to fake, making it a good excuse for the cops to use to insert people who have been flipped and wired back into the group, but just to make you certain you can trust me, the Email I sent you asked you to board the elevator on the sixth floor, but I called you and changed it to the seventh. No one, aside from the two of us would know that, making what floor we should have met on a good test for both of our loyalties and readiness." Both the Asian man and the woman found enough comfort in his words to put their guns away.

A few seconds later the elevator doors opened and a twenty-something Asian woman stepped in. She looked better prepared for a professional woman's fashion shoot than a terrorist attack in her flowing white shirt beneath a light grey blazer and a matching grey pencil skirt with white closed-toed heels and celebutante style sunglasses. Her hair was pulled back and she was carrying her own stylish briefcase, but when the elevator door closed behind her she pulled her hair tie out, fluffed her newly loosened hair, tucked her sunglasses into her briefcase and said, "The mall's a lot quieter than one might think, hey?" The Asian man nodded to her, confirming her as a team member.

"Maybe, but this elevator's full enough." Eric said, confirming in code that the whole team and no one but the team was there.

"Well you would need a chainsaw to cut the tension in here. Are we still a go?"

She asked no one in particular as she kept her back to everyone.

Eric wondered that himself, but said, "We're a go." The woman in red and the Asian man eventually also nodded in agreement.

In the next few seconds, the team aligned so they would be ready to disembark at their floor, the top floor.

The Carlton Tower was the epicenter of business and entertainment for the city and the country. Starting from the bottom, it had a luxurious and massive underground parking lot that expanded into the largest ground level parking lot in the city. The ground level of the building and the next four floors were dedicated to the super mall that

Eric had crossed through. The next few hundred floors were dedicated to business and medical offices and then there was a three-floor condo development that often worked as a hotel for out-of-town visitors. Above that, on the top floor, was the Corrocco Casino.

As one of the largest Casinos in the world, the Corrocco housed double the games of the average Casino. The Corrocco's entire collection of games had a unique vintage design, custom made with only the best materials and the most extravagant craftsmanship. The Corrocco also had a laser tag arena, a rollerblading arena, a separate high stakes card room for big ticket games and their celebrity players, and a club lounge; complete with a full bar, a five star kitchen, a sound stage with instruments and equipment available for rent, and there was a dance floor between the stage and restaurant tables. The restaurant lounge also had its own private VIP area. The entire floor was elaborately decorated as a 1920s speak-easy

    The high-fashion foursome strode quickly through the main gaming area, ignoring the perky crowds, jingling machines, and lit up cash machines. They ignored the crackle of the roulette tables and a particularly excitable group of players that Casino staff had to come up and address. They swiftly made it to the card room.

    The card room was murderously silent in comparison to the rest of the casino which was a welcomed relief for Eric, but still not the finish line. It had white hexagonal tile walls, a dark grey floor of the same tile, and a plain white ceiling with standard florescent bar lighting it was also packed with security officers who stood out shamefully against their light and glamorous backdrop.

As expected, a security guard approached them. The guard was an African man who towered over Eric and had the broadness of a linebacker. They knew he was a security guard by his handsome and solid black suit, name tag, and coiled earpiece. It was clear he was focussed on the red jacketed woman and her baby carriage, but the plan was for her to be distracting; thus far everything was virtually perfect. "Excuse me, Ma'am," the security guard addressed the group in a soft, smooth, and low voice,

"But no one under twenty-one can be in the Casino. You will have to take your baby elsewhere."

"Darrin Folk," Eric lied as he extended his hand for the guard to shake it in a false introduction. "This is Veronica Moore," Eric gestured to the red jacketed woman, "She and her child are invited guests of Mr. Marshall and his party for the meeting in the VIP lounge. I am Ms. Moore's attorney and we're obviously running late."

The security guard's face scrunched. Eric knew that the security guard's confusion was because company policy stated that members of security were to be made aware of any unusual guests such as babies coming to the casino, but Eric counted on the casino staff's commitment to service. "Mr. Corrocco didn't tell us that anyone else was coming," the guard said, playing into Eric's hand, "Or that children would be welcomed at Mr. Marshall's meeting, but the meeting was last minute, so perhaps he forgot to mention it. Come with me." The security guard then led them through the card room, through the restaurant, and into the VIP lounge.

In the lounge, there were six older gentlemen crowding a table packed with spent plates and endless piles of business paper. Eric recognized his target immediately from the red and gold herringbone patterned tie with the distinctive, copyrighted emerald green emblem. There was a security guard in every corner of the room. Both the men at the table and the security guards in the room with them took note of the invading group and Eric's escort was approached by one of the other guards. The two guards whispered amongst each other for a moment telling Eric it was time.

If they waited too much longer, they'd be manhandled and escorted out by security which would make it virtually impossible to take out their target. Before either of the security guards could react, Eric nodded to his team and the shooting started.

Eric fired the first shots, taking out their assigned target and the rest of the men at the table while the rest of the team followed suit systematically. The Asian man shot the rest of the security guards on the floor and the two women began shooting the rest of the restaurant's costumers and staff who were just outside the room. They effectively emptied their weapons that they had kept concealed either in bags or under clothing.

To Eric, it looked as though things were finally going surprisingly well, then he heard a stray shot.

For Eric, it was as though time slowed. He saw the young Asian woman fall to the floor dead, having been shot in the back by one of the security guards that the team thought was already dead. The guard did die of his injuries seconds before anyone fired back at him.

Scarleto had made them all aware of the risk, but losing people on the job was not part of Eric's personal plan. He couldn't help thinking that if Scarleto had let him do things his way; if they had simply skipped the cloak-and-dagger, planted their devices, shot their target, exited, and detonated their devices once they were all at a safe distance; then they would achieve the same results and create less of a mess.

He couldn't dwell on the past though because by now the emergency alarms had been sounding for several minutes and they meant that everyone in the tower was likely being evacuated.

Amid the panic, no one noticed Eric and his team drop their guns where they stood. Eric also discreetly dropped his briefcase next to the body of the dead Asian woman then he and the remaining members of the team then joined the panicked and oblivious evacuees heading down the emergency stairs.

Eric blended into the crowd by helping a young family maneuver the stairs by carrying the youngest of their three daughters in his arms. The rest of the team split away from him as best they could in the tight stairwell. They were not scheduled to meet up again until they were in the getaway vehicle so he put them out of his mind and focussed on wrapping up the mission by escaping.

Carrying the young girl made Eric's every move more difficult and he began to regret offering to help her, but he couldn't leave her to die because there was a chance her family would escape. If they did make it out and she didn't, Eric knew her parents would remember him and hunt for him.

With every move, she felt heavier in his arms. Eric had to keep shifting her from shoulder to shoulder to stay balanced and keep from getting trampled by the title wave of panicked people.

Despite the chaos and his obligation to keep the girl alive through it however, Eric wasn't finished so he eventually managed to stop on a stair. He freed his right hand and removed his cell phone from the corresponding pants pocket. He checked the time on his phone's screen and flashed the nervous toddler his best attempt at a comforting smile, but truthfully what he saw worried him.

They were entering the most dangerous phase of their mission. Here, timing was crucial, but they were already five minutes behind schedule and the crowds that they were hopelessly swept up in were moving much slower than anyone had anticipated when the plan was drafted. Eric knew that making the call he was about to make would probably cost him his life, which was not the plan, but he concluded it had to be done to preserve the mission and cause maximum damage. He pressed speed-dial three on his phone and when a fifth and final team member answered, he breathed one word, "Now."

The last team member was several blocks away waiting in the getaway car, but everyone currently in the Carlton Tower, especially Eric, felt it when he hit his detonator's switch. First, the building shook from above as Eric's briefcase bomb exploded, effectively obliterating the crime scene that the team had made of the Corrocco Casino and its lounge. Then the tower shifted from below as the SUV the fifth team member had rigged to explode and parked in the underground parking lot, detonated. The car bomb was strategically placed so that it would collapse the tower at its foundation and that collapse happened painfully quickly.

Cracks immediately began to crawl over the walls and ceiling of the stairwell causing concrete, marble, and drywall dust to bleed out of the cracks. Between the toddler weighing him down, the shaking of the building, the rushing crowd, and the constantly growing plume of dust; every step Eric took began to feel more like an acrobatic feat, solidifying his belief that he would die here.

Several of the stones that fell from the cracks were large enough to kill which meant that trampled corpses were now among the mounting obstacles for the upcoming steps. Eric was relieved however because as people started dying and the panic thickened, the crowd's pace quickened, bettering his chances of escape.

Eric's reprieve was brief because the situation only worsened from there. Squinting in the dust and stumbling down unpredictable terrain, Eric tripped and nearly fell over a trampled woman's corpse that was now sprawled across the stairs. Eric took a breath as he recognized that if he had fallen, both he and the toddler in his arms would have suffered the same fate that she had. He quickly concluded that it was time to change tactics.

He whispered to the little girl, "Hold on to me tight; as tight as you can!" and when he felt her little arms squeeze his neck more tightly, he jumped over the safety rail. He made it two flights down before briefly settling back on the stairs and then making a second jump. This time he made it three more flights down.

Eric noticed other people start to try and fail at his tactic because they gave their jumps too much lift and were left with nothing but air to grab on to. Hearing their screams as they fell to their deaths nearly a thousand floors below was not saddening for Eric; they were an annoyance.

He made a third jump and made it another two flights, but he felt they were still moving too slowly so he said to the tot, "Really, really tightly now sweet pea." The little girl refastened her grip around his neck and they jumped. This time he held the little girl with only arm and used his other arm to support his descent using the banisters;

similar to how a monkey uses branches to jump from tree to tree.

      Doing things this way, he was able to make it down nine flights in roughly one minute before his arm was too weak to make it further and he melted into the masses on the stairs once again. Ultimately, he had descended approximately nineteen floors in the meager ten minutes since the bombs blew, but even if he could maintain his relatively quick pace, the math he was doing in his head told him he would not make it out. To make matters worse, he now had to consider that the shaking seemed to be worsening and other people that had adopted his jumping method created the added risk of him being knocked down by a careless free-faller.

The walking group Eric was in made it down three more floors before the building really began to crumble around them. The structure moaned loudly before a large piece of steel rebar that was followed by an inordinately large rainstorm of concrete, fell on the crowd. The unexpected collapse created a fence that blocked the path of everyone moving just a few steps slower than Eric, but Eric was not entirely lucky.

A chunk of ceiling support concrete hit Eric hard, cutting him just above his right eyebrow. It dazed and disorientated him briefly and sent blood streaming down his face and creating yet another obstacle for his vision and his escape.

The remaining crowds started moving even faster; making the stairwell even more treacherous, but Eric figured that their speed came too late because soon, the stairs themselves began swaying. Shortly after, whole cases of steps still stocked with people fell almost a thousand floors. The people trapped on those falling stairs were sent to their deaths at the base of the building, but the collapsing of the staircases also prompted Eric to make a last ditch effort to save himself.

"Hold on sweetheart; hold on ok?" The little girl in Eric's arms was crying profusely now because she had been frightened by all the noises of the disaster around her, but she reaffirmed her grip once again. He then jumped over the banister again. This time, he didn't consider the risks of free-fallers because this time he assumed he figured that he was as good as dead anyway so he no longer cared where he landed or whether he even survived the landing.

    Eric fell past thirty floors in a hesitantly suicidal fashion before he remembered that there was a balcony for every exterior room on the fiftieth floor. Eric knew the fiftieth floor was probably still relatively stable given its distance from both explosive devices. He also remembered that it was a very doable jump from any of the balconies to the rooftop of the neighbouring building that would likely be relatively untouched. He'd considered using the balconies as an alternate escape route if things went bad; things were bad. He concluded that emergency escape was his only hope now so he counted the floors more carefully as he continued to fall.

At the fifty-fifth floor, Eric reverted to his monkey climb down the banisters until he reached the fiftieth floor where he backtracked to the emergency exit door, left open by evacuating personnel. He jogged across the floor and made it to a balcony. He then made the final jump from the crumbling balcony to the neighbouring rooftop.

Eric had so many thoughts rolling through his head as he made the leap. He needed the correct form to compensate for the girl's weight and position as he lifted off, floated over the gap between buildings, and landed. He had to ensure he did not land on the girl and he had to land without a crippling injury.

To his disbelief, he landed successfully. He ended up landing on his back. He quickly used his elbows to keep his head from hitting the roof and to stop his momentum from causing him to roll on the girl.

Once he felt stable, he took a moment to catch his breath; he evaluated himself and the girl and concluded the girl was shaken, but fine. He, however, was not so lucky. In addition to some minor cuts and bruising, his right ankle was severely injured. He felt his ankle was broken and he could feel his concussion from the falling roof back in the Tower was worsening. Still, he forced himself to make the mental switch from accepting his death back to action mode.

Fortunately, from where he was, it was an easy climb down the building's exterior fire escape to the ground and once he was on the ground, he could once again melt into the panicked masses; that was exactly what Eric did.

Once he was safe in the crowd, Eric took a moment to appreciate his work. The devastation was more severe than the team had planned and now that he was no longer caught up in it, he was truly thrilled by it. He actually had to cover his mouth to hide the fact that he was laughing.

After his moment of admiration, Eric resumed his fake panic and proceeded to give the girl he'd rescued to a flustered traffic enforcement officer who had been temporarily reassigned to crowd control as more and more people made it outside and more and more curious onlookers clustered around the police barricades. Some people were seriously injured and were stumbling around in shock, others were calling out and actively skimming the crowds for their loved ones; *perfect*. There were also a few others that were simply taking pictures for their most recent social media post.

"Hello," Eric spoke breathlessly to the traffic officer. His voice was barely audible over the sounds of sirens, screams, and the building's collapse so he barely had her attention as he forced the toddler into her arms. "I need you to take this little girl somewhere safe. She isn't mine; I met her family on the fire stairs and thought they might have a better chance of getting out if I carried her, but their other kids slowed them down and we were separated. I don't know if they made it out, but if they did, can you see to it that she gets back to them?"

"Yes, yes sir," the panicked officer said as she took the girl. "Now let's get that head of yours looked at." She then tried to direct Eric to a group of ambulances where paramedics were treating the injured.

He was tempted to accept, but concluded there would be too much risk to the mission so Eric continued his theatrical performance, "No, no," he began spinning and combing his fingers through his hair in a frantic manner meant to indicate he was looking for someone. "I haven't found my girlfriend yet. I was separated from her when I saw the young family. I haven't seen her yet; what if she's still in there?" His eyes welled with tears, but they were caused by the throbbing in his ankle not fearfulness.

"I won't get treatment until I find her." He lied as he strategically wondered away and once he was out of sight, he hobbled the several blocks he needed to and got into the idling silver SUV that was his getaway vehicle.

Inside, the woman in the red jacket and the Asian man were both there, but they were in worse shape than Eric was in and there was no sign of the baby the woman in the red jacket had brought with her. Eric gave the teenage African American boy who was the explosives expert and wheelman a simple order, "Drive."

Eric could tell by his stiffness, facial expression, and cold sweat that the young man had questions, probably about why they were a member short, but he was too nervous to ask. Eric reassured him, saying, "It was a rough mission. Just remember the plan and everything will be ok."

The boy nodded. He continued to seem nervous, but Eric was too tired to be concerned with him further.

As they planned, the wheelman dropped Eric off at his rental apartment and then took the remaining team members to wherever they had preplanned to go. Eric chuckled as he unlocked the door; then laughed out loud as he closed it behind him. He was laughing because he was overjoyed because he had gotten away with mass murder, but the job wasn't done yet. He had a few more calls to make.

Chapter 2

Early that same day, Special Agent Anthony Firestone began the day just like any other day. He got up a half-an-hour earlier than he needed to allow time for the nightshift to update him on what was going on.

He got the coffee perking, shaved, and stepped into a hot shower. When his shower finished, he dressed in a brand new black Armani suit; a new, clean, white shirt; and his favorite solid navy blue tie. Dressed, he made himself a hearty breakfast of bacon and scrambled eggs with toast. Lastly, he flossed, brushed, rinsed with mouthwash, and styled his slowly greying dark brown hair. He then filled a travel coffee mug up with black coffee and left for work.

When Firestone reached his office, he approached the bullpen where his and his partner's desks were. He had an extra bounce to his step. Firestone usually prided himself on being the liveliest and most handsome man in his office. His dark eyes and slowly greying dark hair gave him a mature movie star-like demur that kept the women in the office captivated and his humour created laughter amongst all of his colleagues that often superseded the clamour of ringing phones and negative news reports. Because he was so beloved, he usually approached his work with enthusiasm, but today he was hoping he would see his partner, Leah Fong.

Standing roughly five-feet-three-inches when wearing heels, Leah was a stereotypically perfect Chinese woman. She had a perfectly round face which was encapsulated by her raven black hair that she kept at a length that allowed it to crown her shoulders. When she wore it free, she wore it wavy but she usually wore it tied back tightly.

Firestone was ten years older, a hundred pounds heavier, and nearly a full foot taller than Leah, but he definitely did not see her as being so small because Leah's warrior spirit developed better and when she was younger than most people's did.

When the Fong family emigrated from Shanghai China by boat, Leah was not quite nine years old. She often entertained

Firestone with her stories of learning her first strands of English from the crew on the boat that brought her over, celebrating her ninth birthday on the same boat, and learning a new culture once the boat made it to port; but Firestone also knew her darker stories.

She told him how her mother and baby brother died when the waves from several violent storms weakened and eventually burst through a shoddy weld. The hole caused the boat to flood, drowning them and many others. Firestone also knew that her father had died less than a week later from a cold attributed to getting a chill in the same flood that drowned the rest of her family.

The death of her parents left Leah in the care of her much older brother when she finally arrived in America. Her brother had emigrated a few years previous and was a successful and wealthy lawyer.

Because her brother was so well-off, Leah grew up well fed, beautifully groomed, and in heart-stopping good shape. She kept herself that way into her adult life and all of those attributes came in handy in her chosen career. She also developed a natural taste for getting justice for every victim because her brother had raised her with such a strong respect for the truth and evidence.

Especially considering her upbringing, it was no surprise that Leah had grown up with a tendency to be tough, but fair. She was skilled at reading people and deciding whether she should show toughness or fairness towards them.

She was even more skilled with knives and guns and showed no fear when using them. Leah was skilled at nearly every form of martial arts and hand to hand combat known to mankind. She was brave, bold, smart, and funny as hell. With her by his side, Firestone felt more fearless than usual; without her, he felt the weight of the world on his shoulders.

His heart sunk when he saw that her desk was still sterile. The emptiness meant that Leah had not yet returned from her mysterious undercover mission that was now well into its third month.

Firestone then turned to his own desk which was clear contrast to Leah's as his desktop was so loaded down with teetering piles of folders, files, envelopes, and stray papers that he had to dig through for his keyboard. The only thing left in clear view was a framed photo of Firestone and Leah Fong.

In the photo, Firestone and Fong were both dressed in army greens and were armed with standard assault rifles. Their faces were dirty and shielded by dark sunglasses and hats, but even through that you could see the strength of their partnership and friendship in their body language and smiles. That photo was taken at the end of Leah's first two weeks on the job. Their relationship was strong then and it had only grown stronger since.

The mission they were on when the photo was taken had gone horribly awry and had resulted in Leah getting shot in the shoulder and the target of their investigation, a man named Amilio Scarleto, escaping. Leah had been more able to put many of those negative memories behind her than Firestone, but he let his anger towards himself for letting Leah get hurt and the target escape make him better, more dedicated, and stronger.

Firestone was taking a moment to admire that photo and enjoy his coffee when his Director called to tell him that the Carlton Tower had exploded and he was assigning him to investigate what had happened. Director Meyer was famous for overreacting so Firestone drove to the scene not knowing what to expect, but that changed very quickly.

When he was still miles away, Firestone could see thick black smoke billowing over the roofs of buildings that once surrounded the tower. Firestone remembered that the Carlton Tower was taller than those buildings and appeared like a father lovingly guiding his small children. Firestorm noted that lovely structure could not be seen.

As he got closer, Firestone recognized that the ring of marked asphalt that used to be the above-ground parking for the Tower was now a horribly shredded and spattered mess. The area surrounding the shredded lot was packed with people and vehicles. Many of these were firefighters, local police, and paramedics along with their vehicles. Others were cars that were in the area during the bombing and were now overturned and scorched by a powerful explosive force. Firestone noticed that some the cars were actually stacked on top of each other as if they had been thrown into each other by a cyclone.

As Firestone continued to roll up on the scene he noticed that there was a group of roughly six ambulances at a time lined up just beyond the yellow crime scene tape with an unobstructed route to the highway leading to the hospital. He decided to keep their route unobstructed and parked nearly ten blocks away.

As he walked back up on the scene, he saw more of the devastation and his heart began to pound. Time slowed for Firestone and he became hyper-focussed on whatever details would matter to his investigation.

He jogged past the ambulances on his way under the crime scene tape and barely noticed that their doors were opened to the scene so that they could effectively tend to the relatively minor injuries and transport the wounded who survived more than a few seconds. The moment an ambulance left the line for the hospital another arrived to replace it.

As a result, the smell of exhaust and burning rubber from the ambulances was *almost* strong enough to bury the smells of burning buildings and burning flesh emanating from the still smoldering building.

Once he past the first line of vehicles and barricades, he had a virtually unobstructed view of the building. What was left of the mangled building looked like a surfboard that had been attacked by a shark. It had two definite, jagged gaps that looked like giant bite marks taken out of the foundation on the right side and out of top on the left side.

The 'bite marks' spanned approximately two hundred floors each, but he was only guessing from a considerable distance, he assumed that up close they were much larger.

The entire scene was an astonishing offense to all of Firestone's senses and he had only been there for five minutes.

Firestone's trained mind began to race as he thought about what might have caused that extreme level of damage. He knew that whatever did it was apparently powerful enough to vaporize entire floors of offices and happened quickly enough to trap thousands of people inside the building. There was only one thing Firestone could think of that could cause damage that catastrophic that quickly while still staying relatively contained in two separate locations; *a bomb*; or more accurately, two bombs judging by the damage to the Tower.

    Suddenly, just as Firestone felt he had a good grasp of the devastating scene, the damaged foundation of the tower gave way and what was left of the Carlton Tower moaned, cracked, and crumbled into dust. The dust cloud enveloped the immediate surrounding neighbourhoods in a fraction of a second. Just as the dust cloud was about to overtake him, Firestone could have sworn he heard another blast and then the dust cloud gained momentum. The plume was blinding and suffocating. Firestone was only caught in the plume for less than a minute, but it felt like a lifetime and brought him down to one knee as he choked on the dust, blind.

As soon as the dust cloud passed over him, Firestone tried to see if there was any sign of the second explosion that he thought he'd heard, but before he could make anything out with his watering eyes, he realized that the final collapse of the tower killed hundreds more people and uprooted whatever organization the original scene had and with their deaths. He decided he had to stop searching for something that was probably an echo and do his damnedest to help wherever he could.

The remaining police who were already working the scene shifted to actively working with paramedics and firefighters to separate the wounded from the dead.

Reinforcements arrived to control the crowds and maintain the scene. The barricades that defined the crime scene had to be moved outward because many of the spectators ended up getting hurt in the dust storm. Responders began zipping the dead in body bags and piling them in a nearby alleyway in order to make room for more ambulances. Firestone helped countless wounded people over those next few hours, but one stuck with him more than the others.

She was in her mid twenties and dressed in a navy blue sundress. Firestone found her walking aimlessly around the wreckage of the foundation of the tower on two bloody nubs where her feet once were. She had also violently lost her left arm above the elbow.

As Firestone rushed her to an ambulance, she kept muttering about not knowing where her shoes were and wanting them back because they were a gift from her boyfriend who'd died in car accident a month before. As Firestone watched the ambulance carrying her disappear on route to the hospital at a break-neck speed, he recognized that with the amount of blood she'd lost already, she probably wouldn't make it to the hospital. Although he was not a very religious man, he prayed that her boyfriend would be there for her when her suffering was over.

After several more hours of rescue work, Firestone felt that the scene was sufficiently organized and secured, so he left his number with as many people as possible before he went back to his car with the intention of returning to his office. His thinking was that he would be more helpful processing the evidence that would be flooding in then he would by playing paramedic.

Before he could leave however, Firestone was stopped by a hazmat team dressed in their heaviest gear. They pulled him from his car, stripped him in a hazmat stall. They took his clothes elsewhere while they showered him. About five minutes later, they redressed him in a papery plastic jumpsuit and sent him away in an ambulance of his own.

In the ambulance, he was told by the hazmat-trained paramedics treating him that many of the victims brought to hospital exhibited signs of a rare infection that manifested itself much like radiation poisoning; starting with a sore stomach, heavy sweating, and difficulty breathing which would be followed by a blistering rash appearing on contaminated tissue anywhere from a few seconds to four days after exposure. He was told that if he had an infection that was severe enough, he could be struck down with paralysis or death and that, because the infection was caused by an airborne toxin, it spread much more easily than radiation.

Firestone spent the next two and half hours having tests run on him, swallowing preventative drugs, and receiving vaccines.

After another hour-long wait, his tests came back negative and he was permitted to return to his office under the strictest orders to report any changes in his health directly to that hospital. He proceeded to return to his office and collapsed into his chair.

Thanks to his hectic day, Firestone's hair was left damp and unruly by the shower the hazmat team had forced on him, he could use a fresh shave, and his eyes were bloodshot from the hours he'd spent under heavy stress. His suit had also been exchanged for an agency-issued hooded sweatshirt and sweatpants, but he didn't care about his appearance so much right now. He was still struggling to digest the horrible crime scene he had come from.

To make matters worse, Firestone was forced to recognize that the scene gave him nothing in the way of leads to who was responsible for the devastation.

Everything that had happened that day made him flop down exhausted in his desk chair while aggressively rubbing his tired eyes with one hand and used his other hand to comb through his wet hair.

When he finally opened his eyes, he noticed that several of his colleagues were gathered around his desk and searching for guidance from him, so he climbed up on his desk and loudly said, "As I'm sure you all know by now, the Carlton Tower has collapsed. I can't say with concrete certainty at this point how many people were killed or injured, but I can say we're talking about hundreds of casualties and many of those were first responders that many of us have worked with in the past. We can't rule out anything at this point as far as what caused the fall of the tower, but it sure looks like terrorism."

The word 'terrorism' caused a stir amongst his attentive colleagues, so Firestone waited for the nervous whispers to die down before he continued, "Also, the blast sight produced a dangerous toxin that spreads virulently through the air. It appears similar to radiation poisoning and the boldest signs of it are rashes on the skin, stomach problems, and difficulty breathing."

"Make your families aware of it and keep a close eye on your health and the health your co-workers. Take the sick to Mercy General if you feel they need it, but other than that, stay focussed on your assignments whether it's related to the Carlton Tower disaster or not. We need all hands on deck for this one." He then climbed down and sat back in his chair as the newly-encouraged crowd disbanded.

Once he was alone again, he immediately clutched the framed photo of him and Leah Fong. They were standing in a sun scorched African valley.

When that photo was taken, his hair was still the colour of black coffee. Now the people who knew him well joked it was 'coffee with cream' as more and more grey hairs grew in. He kept his fit frame and slender face, although he had filled out a little with age. Leah, on the other hand, had not changed at all in the ten years since the photo.

He began to rub his eyes profusely again and blindly placed the picture back in its usual corner, but he remained locked into his own thoughts. Firestone could not help remembering the last time he saw Leah. He and Leah were celebrating their perspective birthdays and a send off for Leah's undercover mission on the same night at their favorite Irish and cop bar.

That night, she was wearing a low-necked black dress whose skirt fell loosely just above her knees and open-toed black high heels. She was wearing her hair down and loosely curled. She was also wearing a diamond-look-a-like necklace and matching earrings which added to the sparkle her eyes were already giving off. As he twirled her around to the upbeat rhythm Celtic music he was thinking she was the most beautiful woman in the world.

When he opened his eyes again, he found himself starring at Leah's empty desk and for a moment he actually thought he saw her there. He smiled to himself as he pictured what she would be telling him right now if she was actually at her desk. "C'mon Tony, just because your sexy coffee brown hair is slowly greying, doesn't mean you're ready to retire. You helped dozens of people while the building those people came from crumbled and burned around you; most people would call that amazing, you call it Wednesday. The doctor's say you're lucky to have narrowly avoided a rare infection; I think that's the standard for you. Now answer your phone and get a lead on who's responsible for this."

Firestone snapped back to reality and the illusion of his partner vanished as he answered his ringing phone saying, "Special Agent Anthony Firestone..."

"This is Joan Foster, Sergeant in charge of the Bomb Detection Unit; I'm planning to send you my official report as soon as I can get to my desk to write it, but I figured you'd appreciate hearing my preliminary findings..."

"You assumed correctly," Firestone responded perkily, "Are you and your people alright?"

"Mostly," She said solemnly. "I lost six of eighteen people when the tower finally fell and another was hit with that infection pretty bad. He's in a coma right now and is apparently paralysed from the neck down. Unfortunately, they don't think he'll even wake up at this point..."

"I'm so sorry," Firestone said sincerely, "But you can assure his family that everything that can be done is being done to resolve what's happened here."

"Yes, Thanks," Joan said. Firestone detected a definite crackle in her voice, but passed up the opportunity to console her further. Instead, he politely let her push herself through it and continue her report. "Anyway, getting back to the purpose of my call," she said with a forced chuckle.

"My team and I concluded that there is no way what happened to the tower was accidental because the worst of the damage was concentrated at the foundation of the tower and at the top floors. The middle section of the tower was left relatively unaffected. Something '*natural*' like a gas line explosion, a medical lab accident, or a widespread fire would have either affected the whole building or stay restricted to one relatively small section."

"In the Carlton Tower, we have two separate detonation points and the likelihood of two separate catastrophic events occurring in such a secure and well-built building simultaneously at a time when they maximized damage and casualties..." Joan paused and took a large, loud breath, "Well it's needless to say that the probability of that happening is ridiculously unlikely. The damage done was also clearly explosive. We're looking at the work of two powerful, man-made, and strategically planted devices."

"In addition, we think we know where in the tower the devices were planted because among a lot of other evidence, we noticed some shards from the Carlton Tower's roof on the roofs of neighbouring buildings which suggests that one device was planted in the restaurant area of the Casino on the top floor. When the device detonated, it turned the Tower's roof into a shrapnel shower that coated those other rooftops. Had the bomb been planted much lower there would be shards of the other floors in addition to the roof."

"Also, the device that destroyed the foundation was a large one, planted in the parking garage. We're thinking it was a six-to-eight-seat vehicle that was fully wired and loaded with explosives that are unlike anything we're familiar with. We're thinking that whoever built the devices also made the explosives. If we're correct, than you're looking for an extraordinarily dangerous person or group."

Joan breathed heavily again and took on a traumatized tone as she explained, "The foundation of the Carlton Tower was built with the possibility of multiple vehicles colliding and exploding in flame in mind. A person would need multiple, fully loaded car bombs spaced out throughout the parking garage to damage the foundation the way it was damaged using typical explosives like C4 or an X grade explosive and we're still processing, but we're confident that only the remains of one vehicle are showing to be a car bomb. This tells us that the explosive that was used in that car bomb had at least ten-times as strong blast potential as any known explosive either on the market or in development. We also didn't see any of the standard tags that governments and corporations build into their explosives which helped us confirm it was knew. With that kind of power, the device used to destroy the restaurant might have fit into any woman's purse. It must have been a new kind of explosive; there's just no other explanation."

Firestone felt it was his turn to fuel the conversation, but he had to think hard on what to say next. He knew that the likelihood of pinning down such a unique and undocumented explosive would likely be fruitless, so he felt that having Joan expand on her explanation of it would be a waste of both their time. He decided to turn his attention to the bombers. "There were two devices, so it's conceivable that we're looking for more than one assailant and they are perhaps suffering from the ill effects of the toxin they used to enhance their unique bombs..." He asked cautious.

"Um... actually no," Joan explained with renewed confidence, "The first problem with that theory is, because of all the damage and causalities, we can't rule out a suicide attack; making that ruling is a job for the medical examiner and the rest of the forensic team, so you might have no one to look for. The second problem is that it doesn't look like the toxin was part of the bomb; we think it actually was a side effect of the bomb."

"Explain to me how that's possible, Joan." Firestone said eagerly. He felt that every lead seemed to evaporate as soon as he felt he could chase it which was sickening, but that left him eager to dissect every detail in the hopes of finding something he could use in those details.

"We're still running some intricate tests, but there were stocked science labs, hair salons, pharmacies, medical offices, dental offices, janitor's closets, and literally hundreds of thousands of electronic devices inside. We believe that the blasts mixed the chemicals you'd find in those locations, causing a chemical reaction that created the toxin."

Firestone felt fatigued. In most of the cases, there was a clear victim and a relatively small pool of suspects that Firestone could then narrow further by using what he learned as he investigated, but Firestone knew that with terrorism, there was very rarely just one victim and the cause was rarely clear, so his typical methods for building would not be fruitful. He needed a jumping off point and the scene didn't offer leads, so he began to think differently.

Firestone surmised that, historically, terrorists did not use attacks at the scale of the Carlton Tower bombing to silence an individual, but rather to mark a specific day in history when revenge was taken for an attack that occurred in their homeland or to signify an ideological movement, but there was also a chance that this attack was entirely purposeless and the Carlton Tower could have been targeted for no reason at all.

Firestone thanked Joan for her help and hung up, intending to work his way down his organization's lengthy lists of terror groups and significant occurrences that may have motivated the attack, but as Firestone leaned forward and hung up his own receiver, he noticed the face of a familiar reporter talking on a muted TV screen at the farthest corner of his office. On the screen below her there was a block-lettered headline reading, **'*BROTHERHOOD FOR A PURE AMERICA CLAIMS RESPONSIBLITY FOR CARLTON TOWER DISASTER'.*** Firestone rushed over and turned up the volume. Then he perched himself precariously on the corner of a tipsy conferencing table placed in front of the screen as he steadied every pixel of the report.

Firestone was watching Rebecca Whales; a young, blonde, beautiful bombshell with an impressive history of keeping the facts straight. He had missed a considerable portion of her report, but by the time the news broke for a commercial break, Firestone gathered that Rebecca had received a call from the group calling itself the Brotherhood For A Pure America. They claimed that the Corrocco Casino on the top floor of the tower was one of many businesses they blamed for America distancing itself from the wholesome family values that the country was built on. They also claimed that the shopping center at the foundation of the tower encouraged frivolousness, waste, theft, and plain greed.

The report also promised that more attacks would come if changes weren't made to North America society.

Her report told Firestone that Whales did in fact have an 'in' somewhere. She knew details that no reporter could know since the building collapsed into a shapeless rubble pile within before any media persons had come close enough to get a clear view of the building, but still, Whales knew about the two focussed blast areas and despite Firestone's inner-office pep-talk, terrorism by bomb was not a popular theory just yet *and* what Whales was saying about how the devices were planted was consistent with what Joan had just told him. All of that told him that he had to get the unedited version of what she knew.

If nothing else, she gave him his jumping off point. He immediately called the Cyber unit to get someone to track down a direct number for Rebecca Whales so he could arrange a meeting with her in person and hopefully get some real leads.

As soon as his call connected with cyber; he heard the warm, motherly, and very French voice of Cyber Crimes Specialist Angelique Marceau widening his current break in the case. "Anthony, darling, I've been anxiously waiting to hear from you; come on down and I'll have that reporters number for you plus more."

"I'm already on my way Angelique." Firestone said with a smile as he hung up. Having the spring put back in his step, Firestone decided to forego waiting for waiting for the elevator and jog down the two floors using the stairwell to get to the Cyber Section.

Chapter 3

The Cyber Section was a very modern dungeon. It had eerily smooth walls that were mint green, the ceiling was charcoal grey, and the tile flooring was somewhere in between those two colours. Cyber was kept so dark that it was difficult to see what room you wanted to head into. The darkness was intended to make the computer screens more clear while still reducing the natural draw to make a gaming center out of all the technical gear and vending machines which littered the halls and the rooms. Also, all of the machinery in the Cyber Unit made it uncomfortably hot.

Firestone knew the Cyber Department well and found Angelique immediately. She was a four-hundred-fifteen pound African-American woman. She had crazy curly, black hair with discreet pink and purple streaks mixed in. She was wearing a flattering and climate appropriate outfit that consisted of a hot pink, silk, sleeveless top; a black pencil skirt and thick black heels that clicked and echoed with each step she took.

She marched right up to Firestone, cupped his face in her hands, and pulled him into a lengthy French kiss. Those who could see them stopped to stare. When they finally parted, Firestone kept Angelique clasped in his arms as though they were dancing. "Does your husband know how you feel about me?" He asked; unable to keep a straight face.

Angelique laughed as she took Firestone's hand in hers and pressed a note into Firestone's palm. "We're French," she said with a chuckle, which was a reference to her and her husband's trust in each other and appreciation for affection between friends and family.

Anthony and Angelique were only good friends; both of them understood that and had no interest in changing their relationship. Anthony had a crush on his partner Leah and Angelique was very much in love with her husband, but it was entertaining for them both to get a rise out of the relatively lifeless cyber techs Angelique worked with.

"That is that reporter's number you asked me for," Angelique explained, gesturing to the note she placed in his hand, before Firestone could ask about it. She then led him back to her cubical where blurry images of the Carlton Tower monopolized all three of the large monitors on her sterile desk.

Angelique's chair squealed painfully as her full figure got comfortable inside it then she and Firestone huddled in front of her monitors. "What am I looking at?" Firestone asked.

"This is the reason I wanted to see you in person," Angelique explained. "The video I'm about to show you is actual footage of the Carlton Tower disaster from a few minutes *before* the blast to the present, cut together using footage from nearby surveillance cameras, a police helicopter that was in the area for an unrelated matter, and a few spectators' cameras. Some of the footage is a lower quality due to the impact of the disaster and the quality of camera and there's no sound, but this rendering still paints a clear picture. Brace yourself darling." She hit enter on her single keyboard and the video rolled.

Anthony and Angelique watched uncomfortably as several thousand blurry figures were coming and going from the tower when business was still usual. It was difficult to watch knowing that virtually all of the figures going into the tower were now dead. Still, they did not look away.

About five minutes into the video, Firestone noticed large scores of people pouring out of every exit like ants on a disturbed hill. Several hundred people had evacuated before they saw the top left corner of the tower fragment into shards followed almost immediately by a minor dust cloud blowing up from the parking area at the foundation.

"Wait, Angelique," Firestone instructed calmly. "Can you play it again from the start please?" He clearly had an intense focus on the video so she did what he asked without question so she wouldn't break it. The replay confirmed what Firestone thought he saw the first time, so he had her play it a third time so that he could explain his thinking to her with support from the video.

"There! Stop it there!" He said excitedly, nearly poking her computer screen. With a quick click of her mouse, Angelique paused the video right where Firestone wanted it stopped.

"What are you thinking, darling?" Angelique asked. She was a little startled by Firestone's sudden burst of excitement.

Firestone calmed slightly and gestured to the clusters of crowds at the exits, "Look, Angelique, those people left the building aggressively; it's as if something is already seriously wrong, but roll the tape again please..." She did. Firestone let it roll until after the second impact, the blowing of the foundation, registered. He then had her pause it again to explain, "The devices don't detonate until the evacuation has already been ongoing for several minutes. If the bombs didn't spark panic in the tower, what did?"

Angelique shook her head indicating she did not know what to say. "Play it through," Firestone said. Angelique let the video run until it finished, but other than making Firestone's throat a little dry when the heavier dust plume that had caught him swept over the cameras, he didn't learn anything new from it.

Angelique also shifted her analysis back on to things that were more helpful, "According to the bomb squad; any bag, purse, backpack, or luggage in there is suspect and there are thousands, not to mention the fact that a suicide vest hasn't been ruled out so the video doesn't help us narrow down who our terrorists are, but I do think it helps point to why they attacked..."

Firestone turned his attention back to her with his eyebrows already raised with fully peaked curiosity. Angelique smiled back at him and used her keyboard to rotate the image of the Carlton Tower that was on the central and slightly larger monitor. The rotation placed the focus on the service garage and cemented lot behind the Tower.

Normally, the lot was a space meant for the Tower and the surrounding buildings to dump their excess garbage when garbage pickup was slow. It was also the space where the Tower's delivery trucks came and went.

That day however, that same area had been cleaned up, decorated with inconspicuous potted plants, and was cordoned off with red velvet ropes.

There were exactly three high end town cars and two stretch limousines crowding the lot. A party of five sharply dressed older gentlemen left the vehicles and entered the casino through the service entrance intended for deliverymen. They were welcomed in by another man wearing a noticeable rainbow tie. Angelique gestured to him and explained, "This is clearly something important because that man is Martin Corrocco, the sole owner of the Corrocco Casino and part owner of the entire Tower." Angelique said. "My best guess is that this is a business meeting and rumour has it that the only place Corrocco hosts meetings is in the Corrocco restaurant area..."

"Where the first bombing occurred..." Firestone interjected; sensing her theory and liking it.

"Exactly!" Angelique shouted excitedly. She then pointed out the man wearing the rainbow tie saying, "His wife, Elise Marie Carlton-Corrocco, would probably know what that meeting was about because she is the other owner."

Angelique continued, "Knowing if that meeting was the target may help you narrow down who is responsible because that potentially speaks to motive." She took Firestone's hand in hers again and pressed a second note into his palm. "This is the address of the Corrocco estate. I think you would be wise to meet with Mrs. Corrocco."

Firestone nodded and said, "But I think it would be wise for me to wait until Corrocco is officially declared dead. I'll use the death notification as an excuse to get my foot in that secure door more easily. In the mean time, I'm going to meet with that reporter because I don't want any more vital case information ending up on the air before we can investigate it properly."

"Alright, good luck darling. While you're out in the field, I am going to finish this new code I'm working on. It links satellite data, general web information, and virtually every law enforcement database together into a whole new internet that will process photos. I'm hoping to use it to isolate faces and license plates of vehicles in the Tower. If it works, it will help identify some victims and your terrorists."

Firestone smile enthusiastically and kissed her on her cheek for good luck as he ran out to meet reporter Rebecca Whales.

He heard Angelique's deep, throaty laugh as he climbed the stairs. He loved her laugh. It was contagious, he smiled.

Chapter 4

Thanks to Angelique, Firestone was able to book a private, face-to-face, meeting with Rebecca Whales for a ten O'clock brunch the next morning at a local five-star restaurant called Bella-Notte.

Bella-Notte was an intimate restaurant more famous for its late-night dinners than its breakfast and lunch menus so the restaurant was nearly empty. The emptiness made it easier for Firestone to see Rebecca, but had she not waved shyly when she recognized the waiter was escorting him to her table, he would not have recognized her.

She was dressed in a business-professional and very flattering black dress topped by a dark blue blazer with sparkling gold buttons. Her blonde hair was tacked back in a braided bun, she was wearing wide thick black brimmed glasses, and her signature ruby red lipstick. It was an oddly wholesome look for her since he was used to her prepared-for-TV, dolled-up, and sexualized image.

When he arrived at the table and the waiter left, Firestone showed Rebecca his badge as he shook her hand and sat, "Special Agent Anthony Firestone, thank-you for meeting with me, Ms. Whales."

"It's not a problem," Rebecca said with a smile, "I'm always eager to help members of law enforcement and, please, call me Rebecca."

Firestone smiled back, nodded appreciatively, and explained, "Rebecca, I need you to understand that everything we discuss here today has to remain off the record, at least for now."

"Absolutely," Whales said with a nod. "I never bring details to the news desk without expressed written permission from everyone reachable involved. Besides, I'm a little freaked out by this one and wouldn't mind distancing myself from it."

"I'll do my best to make that happen, but first, I need you to tell me exactly what you know and how you know it." Firestone said in an authoritative and comforting, almost fatherly tone.

Whales nodded and explained, "We heard about the blast the moment it happened. The news room has police scanners and hundreds of people phoned in. My producer Brian screened all the calls that came in for information to beef up the broadcast, but somehow the guy slipped through his screening to my direct line."

"Do you know how he was able to do that?" Firestone interrupted as he took notes.

When Whales answered, she sounded embarrassed. "I give hundreds of business cards out a day; most are the cards that the station printed for me, but others are ones with just my direct line that I make myself. The more personal cards are for the people

Brian would be forced to deny my talking to. This is the first time in my career that I'm actually concerned about who can reach me."

Whales paused briefly to take a sip of ice water before she continued, "He spouted that babble that I said on the air about America's values being ruined by businesses like the Carlton Tower that promote wasteful spending, greed, and sexuality. I was about to write him off as wacko and hang up, but he then described details about what had happened that only the bomber could know."

"Like what?" Firestone asked before he sipped from own glass of ice water.

"Like that there were two devices; one was planted in the Corrocco Casino's

Restaurant. The other was placed in a Suburban vehicle and parked in the underground garage."

"He also explained very technically how the bombs were built, their sizes, and that they were made with homemade explosives that his group made themselves."

A waiter then approached their table. It was mandatory when in a restaurant like Bella-Notte to order food when you were occupying one of their tables for more than ten minutes and it was clear that their conversation was going to go well beyond that line so they ordered. Firestone ordered a chicken cord-au-bleu sandwich with vegetarian ravioli on the side. Rebecca Whales ordered tomato bisque and a side of egg whites and a lemonade. Firestone stuck with water.

As soon as the waiter left with their orders in hand, Firestone rebooted their discussion, "There were secondary complications for us immediately after the blast so our initial findings can't be confirmed for another few days yet. How did you know that what he was telling you was worth listening to?"

"I have other sources in law enforcement that I had literally just hung up with. What he said fit with what I was just told by my experts."

"I need to know exactly what they said to you." Firestone instructed.

She nodded and brought her large, brown, briefcase-style purse from the floor to her lap. She took a second to rifle through its contents before pulling out an encased CD. She said, "I thought you might. When I realized the caller wasn't a wacko, I had the call recorded. This is everything the recorder caught; all the technical stuff is on there, but I had to sneak it out without Brian knowing." Firestone reached for the disk, but she withheld it mischievously.

In an instant, her wholesomeness evaporated into the precise and ambitious image Firestone was used to seeing on his TV screen. "You understand I could lose my job over this, right? If it comes out that I actively work with police, I will never get another informant. Not to mention, my producer

Brian is ruthless and his whole face glowed when he heard the recording played out loud because he recognized that this is the holy grail of exclusives. It has a terrorist's actual voice recorded and gives unique insight into the devices. This is also the original and only copy."

"In Brian's mind handing it over to anyone compromises its exclusivity. He thinks I'm meeting with you to build on my exclusive and he's going to be mad enough when I refuse to build on the report. Once he realises the disk is gone, he'll know I gave it to you and he will be mad enough to fire me for sure, so if you want this disk I need two things."

"One, I need you to promise me that you'll do your best to make sure that as few people as possible know that this evidence came from me."

Firestone nodded, but he was chewing his lip in uncertainty and frustration. He could not guarantee her anonymity because of the sensitive and urgent nature of what was happening, but he didn't tell her that and she continued, "The second thing I want is the exclusive. Keep the disk hidden and keep me in the loop. If something in this investigation should air, I get it first."

"I guess that's fair," Firestone said hesitantly, "but I came here with a slightly risky favour to ask you that won't mix well with your first demand…" He said.

Her eyes brightened and she slowly slid the disk across the table, giving it to Firestone, "Go on..." She prompted eagerly.

Firestone waited for the approaching waiter to distribute their food and leave again before he explained, "I need you to bait a trap for this guy by telling a bit of a lie on the air. It will put you in real danger and will cost you some credibility, but it is our best chance of catching theses terrorists"

Whales was now donning a full-blown smile and was practically drooling at the concept, "I'm in! Tell me what you need and it will be on the noon *and* six O'clock reports; with this, that disk will be as good as garbage to Brian. Who knows, he may even nominate me for an award."

Firestone nodded and explained, "I need you to plead with the caller for a face-to-face interview. If he accepts and agrees to meet, myself and a small group of plain-clothed officers will follow you to the meet and apprehend him as soon as he can be identified." He then went into more detail of how the trap would work.

Whales was on board and had her producer, Brian, on board as well before they had even managed to finish their meal. After that the plan seemed to roll like a well-oiled machine.

Chapter 5

Rebecca's plea aired at noon. By fortunate coincidence, Eric Bell had taken a break from packing up his rental and was enjoying a platter of microwaved leftovers when he saw it. He had intended to simply admire his handiwork that was now playing out on live television. It was now almost a full two days since he and his team had destroyed the Carlton Tower and the media had everything they were going to get from him, but her plea gave him an idea for something else.

The day of the blast, Eric called Rebecca Whales as soon as he was securely sitting where he was seated now, and because of that, Rebecca and her team were now constantly center stage reporting the story. He had meant for that to be the case because he knew that she often had the majority of the public by the throat, which meant she would likely get them the most attention; but foremost to Eric was his almost uncontrollable sexual attraction towards her. His feelings made him enjoy watching her more than he enjoyed watching any other reporter.

Of course, she had no idea he existed and would probably run from him if they ever did meet, but if he ever could get her alone, she would be his. As a result of his feelings, watching her reports was his porn.

Eric's smile widened more and more as he watched Rebecca's blonde curls bounce up and down on her shoulders and across her large breasts; drawing attention to them because the neckline of her hot-pink dress was so revealing that her breasts could almost pass for bare.

Rebecca explained that the confirmed death toll after the blast and corresponding collapse was ten-thousand-seven-hundred-twenty-four. Three thousand more people had since died from either their injuries or ill effects from the rare toxin; making the total death toll of the Carlton Tower disaster around fourteen thousand with the promise of more to come.

Eric's smile faded slightly as Rebecca went into more detail about the virulent and lethal toxin. He had not planned for it. In fact, he did not know about it and now his dream girl was telling him that he was potentially lethally infected by it. He had multiple, large patches of irritated skin on various parts of his body, his nose, mouth, and chest burned with each breath, he was losing some hair, and was often dizzy. Prior to hearing what Rebecca had to say, he assumed he was suffering from some minor injuries sustained while evacuating the tower along with allergies and stress.

His demeanor changed again however when she drifted back her plea, "With the promise of more attacks, I think I speak for everyone in the country when I say you got our attention with the first. We can all agree that America is changing and that not all of the changes that have happened have necessarily been good. Perhaps other changes need to be made in order to right some wrongs that have been done, but if you truly intend to make America stronger than you should plead your case in a more civilized manner. Tell us what we need to do. That is how you influence the powerful and the masses equally; violence is the wrong approach."

"I hope I'm not arrogant in assuming the fact that you called me means that you trust me to tell your story the right way, so I'm proposing you meet with me. Please, give yourself the opportunity to gain support for your cause without any further bloodshed."

Eric was not a terrorist. He was hired to execute a target and follow a pre-laid plan to disguise that execution as something that would be impossible for law enforcement to work through. He had no interest in building an army for a cause he couldn't care less about. He had even less interest in putting himself out there for the world to see and possibly identify, but he thought about the fact that his rental was virtually packed up. His plans to leave were already in place and now he was presented with an opportunity to make his greatest wet dream come true before he disappeared. This meet Rebecca was asking for was his opportunity to get her alone and get what he really wanted from her.

He called her and arranged to meet her for coffee on the outdoor patio of a small cafe across town, near the newsroom. She agreed to his terms and set the meet for three O'clock that afternoon so that his response to her plea could air at six O'clock that evening.

Undisclosed to Eric, Whales then relayed those plans to Firestone who quickly got a team together and set up his trap at the cafe.

Eric, who was still unknown to Firestone and Whales, had established that he would be wearing a black T-shirt, white kakis, a denim jacket, and a green rimmed denim baseball cap, so everyone knew who to look for at the cafe.

At ten minutes to three O'clock, Firestone stood with Whales, passing himself off as a cameraman while another two plain-clothed agents pretended to be a loving couple enjoying some window shopping across the street. A small team of uniformed officers were also inconspicuously circling the surrounding five mile radius in case their man managed to slip through the immediate team's fingers.

Then Eric Bell approached.

Whales was the first to spot him. He had not yet entered the patio when she all-too-boldly pointed him out to Firestone. There was a brief moment where Firestone and Bell simply stood starring at one another.

Bell was slack-jawed. He immediately saw through Firestone's cameraman disguise immediately and he was angry at himself for letting his most primal urges lead him into a trap.

Firestone could make out Bell's startled expression even at the distance they were and he knew that their cover was blown. "He made us," Firestone discreetly explained to his team through the coiled ear piece he was wearing, "Let's move in."

Firestone stayed still; he was hoping not to shift Bell's star struck state, but Bell was better than Firestone had hoped.

Bell's trained and experienced mind clicked into place faster than most people's would have and he immediately assessed his competition. Firestone was older than he was, but not by much. He looked to be the same height, but he was built very well. Bell determined that Firestone had a wide but sleek runner's build enhanced with a solid muscle tone. Bell guessed Firestone would be a great runner and an even better brawler. Eric also understood that, in his sickened state, he would be no match for Firestone, so he banked on the current distance between them as his only hope of escape.

That hope dimmed however, when he caught sight of the couple on a stealth approach towards him from across the street. Although they were dressed like average Joe`s and had no visible identifiers such as badges, guns, or ear pieces; Eric *knew* they were cops. He also knew they were about to close the all important gap between him and Firestone.

Then, yet another stroke of luck came Eric Bell's way. An SUV came speeding down the street, temporarily trapping the plain-clothed officers on the opposite sidewalk. Eric took the split-second opportunity to turn and run.

Bell heard the cops yelling after him in a chaotic and inaudible cacophony of "Police, Federal Agents, freeze! You are under arrest! Stop him!" Bell glanced back briefly; long enough to gather that it was the undercover couple doing all of the yelling. Firestone was simply running after him and closing the gap quite efficiently.

Bell guessed that by now dozens of nearby cops would have heard his description and direction of travel thanks to the communication devices the trap team had on them. He predicted he had less than a minute before he would be hopelessly surrounded by law enforcement. If that happened, he would surely be arrested because he was unarmed and losing his strength rapidly.

His lungs were burning, his nose was beginning to bleed, and his eyes were now watering in a painful and blinding fashion. That damned infection; it had him in a death grip.

Suddenly, Bell snapped back to reality and assessed his surroundings again. Shockingly and to his relief, Bell knew this street well. He knew there was an inconspicuous construction site at the end of a nearby shadowy alleyway. Bell turned into the alleyway, ran through, and slowed as he approached the site.

Bell glanced behind him quickly. He noticed that his quick dash into the alleyway had successfully widened the distance between him and his pursuers, but he recognized that it would only be seconds before someone realized the route he had taken and were on him again.

Eric needed a break from running in his weakened state, so combat being hunted down, he grabbed a workman's jacket that had been left unattended on a chair next to a table loaded with tools and other gear intended for site volunteers.

He utilized that table and switched his cap for a hard hat, put on a tool belt, the jacket, and work boots. He then strode into the site as if he were about to help frame the wall, but he had been sloppy.

Bell had left his identifiable gear on the table where he had switched it for the construction gear he was currently wearing, so when Firestone finally stumbled on to the site and saw Bell's clothes on the table, he knew to give everyone on the site a hard look. It took Firestone less than one adrenalin-fueled minute to recognize Bell's dirtied kakis. Firestone cautiously stalked his target, hoping to take him by surprise.

Bell was too hopped up on his own adrenalin however to be snuck up on. He saw Firestone coming and went into a full sprint, continuing into the next phase of his escape.

He had another apartment in the area that was listed under a different identity than his packed up and prepped rental.

Fortunately for him, Bell had managed to steal a few minutes of rest while blending into the construction site; Firestone did not have that luxury and now the strain on his muscles was dragging him down which allowed Bell to strengthen his lead significantly, despite his heavier clothing.

Eric took one last look behind him to make certain the coast was clear before he took the final step of climbing the fire escape latter up to his apartment window. He kept that window permanently wedged for times like this when easy entry was a life-or-death kind of necessary, but because law enforcement would be hot on his trail now; he removed the wedge once he was safely inside because he would be leaving this city soon, making that escape route void anyway, so he did not want the wedge to draw attention to his apartment.

As he removed the wedge, he saw Firestone jog up the street and scan the buildings, so Bell froze. Bell barely let himself breathe because he knew that Firestone was looking for him and that he would likely notice a shift in the shadows in any apartment window if there was any movement. Bell was confident that he had escaped; all he had to do was remain still.

Firestone found himself at the heart of an octagonal cul-de-sac made up of rundown apartment buildings, abandoned warehouses, and two no-tell motels. Firestone was angered because he knew that his target could have gone into any of the buildings he was looking at. All of the buildings had decaying brick walls and entrances that Firestone hesitated to utilize without back up and a vest. All of the buildings also had most of their windows either boarded or broken making them even more difficult to judge what was inside.

    Out of energy and with very little hope of seeing and apprehending his target through all the obstructions in his path, there was nothing left for Firestone to do but hopelessly scan the unobstructed windows for some sort of sign while catching his breath.

Then, Firestone's phone rang. The caller was Angelique; she was confirming that Martin Corrocco was officially dead, having been identified at the morgue. That meant that Firestone now had a legitimate reason to breach the Corrocco estate that the Corrocco family legal and security teams could not argue with. He could then ask Mrs. Corrocco about the potentially targeted meeting he and Angelique had found.

Firestone reluctantly accepted that leaving here to go and talk to Corrocco's widow was the wisest move for him to make, but while he had Angelique on the line, he gave her his location and told her to dispatch enough officers there to search each building thoroughly. He also had her compose a computer generated 'sketch' of Bell.

Bell was elated to see his pursuer walk away with a defeated slump to his shoulders, but he had recognized Firestone was on his phone and assumed that the hunt was not over yet. Firestone and Bell did not know each other just then, but Eric Bell vowed that he would learn the name of the man who had come the closest yet to arresting him. Bell imagined that Firestone was feeling just as passionate about putting a name to *his* face as well. Bell was becoming absorbed in the thrill of Firestone's chase.

He was too thrilled, in fact, to realize that his nose was still bleeding.

Chapter 6

Early the next morning, Firestone hung up from yet another call from Angelique as he stopped at the rustic iron gate protecting the lengthy driveway of the Corrocco estate. She told him that the full quarter of the city had he had lost his terrorist suspect in was locked down five minutes after Firestone had called her and eight teams of twelve officers each had been dispatched to the octagonal cul-de-sac that was the last place Firestone had seen his terror suspect. They systematically converged on all of the buildings in that cul-de-sac and arrested everyone, but Firestone's suspect was not among them.

It was not a total failure, however, because one of the property owners did confirm that he had rented out an apartment to the man in Firestone's sketch and although the apartment was empty, they did find a blood trail that led from where the chase first began to right inside that apartment. Unfortunately, the personal information on the leasing agreement was false, but Angelique explained that forensics was being run on the blood and that she was waiting to hear from a Detective Donna Sparks for the results.

Angelique's phone call should have energized him, but Firestone was simply frustrated that he had not noticed the blood trail. He felt that, had he seen it, he would have followed and potentially apprehended his suspect. Now he had to trust some no-name overworked detective would get done what he should have done.

That frustration was what was on his mind as he turned his attention back to the extremely upper-class Corrocco estate. He forced himself to focus on how he was here today to hopefully uncover the purpose of the clandestine meeting between Martin Corrocco and the several, as yet unidentified, businessmen. Firestone recognized that deconstructing that meeting could be crucial the Carlton Tower disaster investigation.

He took a deep breath to calm himself and pressed the call button on the speaker box connected to the gate. He identified himself as a Federal Agent and held his badge up to a nearby surveillance camera. Once the security guard's voice coming from the other end of the speaker acknowledged his identification, Firestone explained his need to speak with Mrs. Corrocco. The security guard muttered a somber, "Yeah, C'mon in." A loud and lengthy buzzer went off and the gate screeched open.

Firestone was impressed by the nearly one mile long, winding, paved driveway that spanned from the main roadway just ahead of the gate all the way to the Corrocco's front porch. The roadway divided two fabulous, clean, white, fenced horse corrals. Every horse was either a world class racer, a trophy winning show jumper, or a certified bloodline breeder and their high-class nature was maintained well in their professionally kept several hundred acre pastures.

After rounding the last wind of the driveway, Firestone was taken aback by the impressive mansion. It seemed to crop up out of nowhere, having been concealed by well pruned trees and hedges bordering the driveway and corrals. The building looked more like a high end country club than a home.

It had a stretched out, two story design with clean white siding, black shutters, black porch wood, grey shingling, and regal looking white marble pillars. He pulled his government-issued black sedan up next to a red and gold antique model-T and respectfully walked across the porch up to the grand oak French-style front door.

He rang the doorbell while showing his badge to the over head security camera and a rapidly aging woman with swollen, red, and teary eyes opened the door a crack. She was wearing her curly, greying-black hair unfashionably short and she was wearing a black sequinned dress that looked better suited for a much younger woman.

"Elise Corrocco?" Firestone asked as he adjusted his badge so that it was in her sightline instead of the camera's, "I'm Special Agent Anthony Firesto..." Before he could finish his introduction, she ran at him hard and collapsed into his arms, sobbing.

"Oh officer," she moaned between sobs, "I thought it would take longer, but you have me. You know I'm responsible for everything. Take me away."

Firestone just stood there and stared at nothing in particular, stunned.

When his shock finally melted away, Firestone's mind was bombarded with questions. *What had she meant when she that she was responsible for everything? Had Elise Corrocco somehow orchestrated the Carlton Tower disaster and the demise of her husband? If so, how had she done it and why?*

Without saying a word, Firestone freed his handcuffs from his belt and used his strength to adjust Mrs. Corrocco so he could cuff her properly. Before he could click the cuffs into place, a meek man's voice said, "Hey, whoa, what do you think you're doing?"

Firestone looked up quickly to see a small man standing in the doorway. He looked like he was in his late sixties, standing only about five feet tall. He had a horse-shoe shaped ring of auburn hair that was clearly dyed that colour; he wore gold rimmed round glasses, a neatly pressed black penguin suit with a blue and white checkered shirt beneath the vest. He also wore a too-tightly-tied red and white polka-dotted bowtie. "Why are you putting the lady of the house under arrest?" The little man urged angrily.

"She has admitted responsibility to a crime and wants to be arrested. Procedure demands that I bring her back with me for further questioning." Firestone explained calmingly.

"Bully your procedure," The man said; turning tomato faced and letting a well-hidden British accent shine through. "Madam Corrocco is clearly disturbed by the loss of her husband and the rest of her guests that were at her tower. She is so distraught, in fact, that she doesn't know what she's saying. I'm Marc Perkins, chief legal counsel for the Corrocco family. Get inside and I will answer whatever questions you may have." The little man led the way inside.

Firestone mentally growled. He did not like drifting from procedure and he especially hated it when the demand to drift came from a lawyer, but he was forcibly directed by his superiors to treat the widow Corrocco with the upmost respect, so he reluctantly removed the handcuffs and respectfully guided Mrs. Corrocco back inside.

Firestone was surprised by what he saw inside the Corrocco mansion. When he first stepped in to the manor he was walking on seamless, freshly finished white marble tile with impressive veins of grey and the occasional sparkly flake, but a person would expect no less than that lavish perfection in a mansion such as this; the surprising part was the fact that this impressive tiling only spanned the dimensions of a standard powder room before it transitioned into a standard shine-finish dark hardwood floor that flowed into an open-plan living room, dining room, and kitchen. The lavishness had given way to an unexpectedly homey atmosphere.

The furniture in the living room was a durable and comfortable brown suede that Firestone felt he could someday have in his own home if he ever settled into a place for more than six months. The walls were painted a soft red and were covered with antique looking erotic art that seemed to clash with the welcoming and homey style of the rest of the house.

After he politely waited for Elise Corrocco to sit in her rocking chair, he took a seat on the sofa across from her. Firestone turned slightly so that his attention could stay with Perkins who continued on into the kitchen still talking, "I assume you are here to tell us that Martin is, in fact, dead?"

Mrs. Corrocco squealed painfully and brought the box of tissues from the glass-topped coffee table to her lap and then took one to dap her dripping eyes. "Yes," Firestone said regretfully. He reached over and caressed Elise Corrocco's hand in his, "I'm sorry for your loss ma'am."

She nodded, used her free hand to maneuver a tissue to collect all of the teardrops streaming down her face. Once her cheeks were dry, she said a very solemn but sincere, "Thank-You." Her lawyer, however, was a lot calmer and brighter.

"Well it's not as though we didn't see this coming, is it, Elise? Would you like anything to eat or drink, detective?"

Firestone really wanted a coffee, but he made it a point never to accept consumables from interviewees so he simply said, "Uh, no thank-you and I'm a Special Agent not a detective." As Firestone spoke, Perkins rejoined the group carrying a trey with a steaming antique white teapot with a flowering peach tree painted on the sides and two matching teacups. There was also a bottle of prescription medication in the heart of the trey.

Without acknowledging Firestone further, Perkins set the trey down on the coffee table and picked up one of the teacups. He filled it with tea and handed it to Mrs. Corrocco. He explained, "First we heard that the tower had been destroyed, then when nearly a day passed without a word from Martin..." Perkins stopped himself as he caught sight of his distressed client through the corner of his eye and spoke more softly, "Well as unfortunate as it was, it didn't take much more for us to realize what had happened. Your eucalyptus and Moroccan spice tea with milk, honey, and one spoonful of liquid sugar; madam." He then gave her a pill from the prescription bottle, saying, "This will help you feel better." He presented each similarly to how Firestone imagined an Arabian servant would serve his Sultan.

Before Firestone could object, Mrs. Corrocco swallowed the pill and washed it down with a cautious sip of tea. This action frustrated Firestone because he recognized that medications have a tendency to muddy the mind and tire the body. He bet that he only had about ten minutes to extract meaningful information from the widow Corrocco before she would need to lie down and he would be escorted out.

His trained mind then flashed back to his first few moments on the property and the widow Corrocco's admission of guilt. He could not stop himself from wondering if Mrs. Corrocco's pill taking was by design.

"I assume you're still here because you have to do your due diligence, right?" Perkins started up again and before Firestone could acknowledge that fact, he blathered on, keeping his back to Firestone as much as possible. "You need to know where we've been, our possible motives and so on; which I think is ridiculous because the news is saying that a terrorist group is claiming responsibility for the entire disaster and the very suggestion that Madam Corrocco would have any involvement with such people is absolutely…"

"That's quite enough, Marcus." A subdued Elise Corrocco interjected; she took a heavy gulp of tea before continuing on to explain, "If Martin were here instead of me, I'm certain that he'd want my death investigated thoroughly, no matter what the news says. Let the man ask what he needs to ask."

Firestone perked up for the first time in a while as though he was finally getting real traction, then Perkins struck up again, effectively pissing on his campfire, "Alright then," the small man puffed; clearly irritated, "Mrs. Corrocco loved her husband passionately and the tower made her millions a year. This disaster not only took the man she loved away from her, but also will likely cost her *billions* in repairs and restructuring. Not to mention that bringing those billions of Carlton Tower guests endless hours of enjoyment was Madam Corrocco's only reason to get up out of bed in the morning. If she *were* to be involved, she would have hurt her herself more than anyone else, except for maybe me."

Firestone raised his eyebrows and the little man clarified his most recent statement, "When the Corrocco's lose money and business, I lose money business. I am the only lawyer in my one-man-boutique-firm and the Carlton and Corrocco families are my only two clients. Martin was the last surviving Corrocco, so without him, I've lost half my firm."

Firestone was having a hard time being empathetic. He knew that the manner-lacking bastard of lawyer still would make more in a month than most people would make in a year and still he seemed to care more about his bottom line than the lives that were lost.

Firestone thought back to the young woman who had lost her feet in the disaster and struggled to stop himself from tearing the man a new layer of skin. Firestone's lower lip hurt from being bitten down on so hard and he could feel that his face had severely reddened.

Perkins, no doubt sensing Firestone's rage, bolstered his argument with a relevant change in subject, "As far as alibis are concerned, Mrs. Corrocco and I have been here together all week. We've been working from about nine in the morning to nine at night with the rest of the legal team ironing out the terms of the sale of the Carlton Tower."

Firestone perked again; he pulled the surveillance photo of Martin Corrocco ushering the, as yet, unidentified businessmen into the tower via the service entrance that he got from Angelique and placed it on the coffee table for Corrocco and Perkins to analyze. "So this then," Firestone deduced, "Is related to that sale?"

Perkins nodded and, more respectfully, elaborated. "This meeting was the sale. The Corrocco's felt that it was important, since the Carlton Tower has always been family run and largely family orientated, that they should get to know the potential buyer or buyers on a personal level and hopefully ensure that those personable values will always be respected. The other gentlemen you see in this photo were supposed to bid on and ultimately buy the tower, spicing their offers with their ideas on how to tower's personable values would be integrated once they gained control."

Firestone treaded carefully, "Their bodies haven't been identified yet, do you know their names and how we can get in touch with their next of kin?"

Perkins initially shook his head, but then he backtracked, "They are all either from out of town or out of country, but I'm certain we have some legal documents that feature their names and corporations. I will make those available to you."

Firestone nodded and, recognizing that Mrs. Corrocco was now flushed and tipsy looking, said, "Lastly, do you have any reason to suspect that Martin Corrocco or this meeting may have been targeted?"

Immediately, Perkins shook his head; he was probably planning to deflect back to the popular belief that the whole mess was a random act of terrorism, but Elise Corrocco shouted, "YES!!!" Her shout was so loud and so sudden that it caused both men to nearly jump out of their seats.

She started sobbing again, "Oh, my husband made *so many* people *hate* him." She sniffed violently, "I couldn't let him ruin my name, my life, or my business anymore. That's why I did it; that's why I did it all. Oh, all those people shouldn't have died. I'm *so* sorry. I'm so *tired*."

Firestone jumped up; but yet again, Perkins intervened. "Clearly the mistresses' medication has taken over; I should put her to bed. Have you got everything you need for the moment?"

Firestone objected profusely; he felt that the lady Corrocco needed to be arrested and questioned further, but before he could even do anything more, two brawny security men barged in from out of nowhere and practically carried him out to his car while Counsellor Perkins took Elise Corrocco in the opposite direction deeper into the house. The security men kept Firestone surrounded until he got into his car and began to head back down the driveway.

Firestone smacked the steering wheel hard with his palm and growled simultaneously as he drove. Firestone's career had been built by the promise that money does not buy justice; and yet, there was money buying justice as clear as he had ever seen it. He knew for a fact that had Elise Corrocco been anybody else, anybody without a high priced and borderline corrupt lawyer, anybody without friends in high places, and without ballsy security prepared to blur whatever just lines may remain after the others were through; she would have been on the other side of his interrogation table. She was not anybody else though. She had the lawyer, the security, and the friends so if he had brought her in, Perkins would simply have argued with the same fluff he had pushed Firestone away with, proceed to butter it up with some name dropping, and one of Firestone's superiors would have released her and he would have likely been reprimanded.

Still, knowing that the effort would have been wasted did not make the action of not doing it any easier to swallow and he knew his investigative interest was piqued. He knew it would remain piqued until the air was properly cleared.

Finding out what the widow Corrocco really felt guilty about was the only way he could clear his mind.

Chapter 7

Eric Bell was hurriedly packing up the remains of his entire life in this city into his set of new plain-black luggage while forcibly arguing with Amilio Scarleto over the phone. "Respectfully, you drew up this plan. We merely carried it out as you instructed us to do *AND* you hired us *BASED* on our reputations for causing as much destruction as possible; that includes maximum body counts. Everyone involved here knew the risks. I WILL NOT be held responsible for the deaths and injuries suffered by my crew."

Eric barely listened to Scarleto's return argument as he continued to pack because he knew that Scarleto was losing his mind. Eric got wise to Scarleto's mental struggles when he rehearsed Scarleto's plan for the fall of the Carlton Tower on his home simulator before they acted on it. Eric detected the flaws in the plan that he struggled with on the simulator, but when he brought his concerns to Scarleto's attention, Scarleto through a childish tantrum and demanded that the mission go his way in a clearly-crazed fashion.

Now, Scarleto had forgotten that he himself had established that there was a strong likelihood that every person on Eric's team may die during the mission.

Despite his disinterest, Eric clued in to the last line of Scarleto's argument, "I had hoped to be able to reuse you and your team as good help is hard find, especially these days."

"No one knew that the toxin would be created." Eric continued to explain himself in an effort to calm the irrational and dangerous Scarleto. As he talked, Eric scratched a irritated rash patches on the back of his neck among other places. His condition was worsening. He tried to ignore it and continued, "Even without the toxin though, we both knew that we should expect a minimum of one casualty following the explosion. I think it's lucky that we were able to keep the loss of life to that minimum."

"You may have suffered only one casualty in the tower, but that hot package with the fuzzy red coat has since died, so what you are saying is *unacceptable* to me. I have no doubt that you've heard the stories of those before you that handed me unacceptable results."

Eric had heard every horror story related to Scarleto, but he felt that no torture could be as painful as that conversation, so he endeavored to wrap it up and finalize his escape. "The way I see it, this entire conversation is a waste of both of our times; not to mention it creates an unnecessary and risky link between us. I'm sorry you are unhappy with what happened at the tower, but the target was eliminated and every trace of our true purpose was buried in the blast like you wanted; the mission was a success."

"Was it really? That Agent, that one you seem to like so much, came dangerously close to *both* of us."

"*Firestone*," Bell interjected, "His name is Anthony Firestone and I do not like him, I respect his work ethic. It takes a special person to get as close to me as he has..."

"I know all about Firestone," Scarleto said, "He's the reason I'm the one planning from a distance and calling the shots over the phone instead of being in your place." Eric was surprised.

Scarleto took a deep, frustrated breath before he explained his thinking further, "I instructed you to attack now because Firestone's partner is currently out of his reach. As good as he is, she's better. I thought that the working without her combined with the increased trauma of the Carlton Tower event would have put him out of commission, meaning that someone less competent would be on your tail by now, but I see that Firestone is still a force not to be underestimated."

"Well I'll make sure I don't underestimate him then. Would you like me to hunt that partner of his down; perhaps her death will distract him."

"That's not a half bad idea actually, Mr. Bell."

"What did you call me?" Bell asked while failing to hide how shaken he was because, until then, Scarleto new him as Eric Johnson, not Eric Bell.

Scarleto let loose a light but maniacal chuckle before he said, "I know everything there is to know that is worth knowing, young man, and that includes Firestone's partner's current whereabouts. You had better leave Leah to me. She and I have a special connection and you've already muddied things up enough."

Bell raised his free fist in frustration as he said through clenched teeth, "You're the one who made the overly complicated plan and what's worse is that because of what's happened here, I had to give up both this rental, which I planned, but also my emergency apartment in the development zone which I needed not only for this job but for others like it as well. I had to cut my connection with that apartment because

Firestone saw me go into it and got some lackeys to comb the area. I narrowly escaped by taking the fire escape out, but you have essentially cut away my safety net and now you're wasting my time *and* putting me at more risk by calling me and giving me shit about things that ARE OUT OF MY CONTROL!"

His client responded in kind, "IT WAS YOUR OWN ARROGANCE IN THINKING THAT YOU COULD RAPE THAT REPORTER THAT PUT FIRESTONE ON YOUR TRAIL AND COST YOU YOUR SO CALLED SAFETY NET! AS FAR AS THE PLAN IS CONCERNED, WE BOTH KNOW THAT YOU COULD HAVE STRAYED FROM IT!"

Bell quickly realized that this game of spreading blame that they were playing was doomed to lead nowhere good, so he chose to ignore Scarleto's most recent rebuttal and continued his own rant, only more intellectually. "Moreover, I have already declined payment and therefore whatever inconveniences you have suffered should be taken as acceptable losses in my opinion. You should know that I will not expect or accept any further communications from you because the risk is too great for all involved, agreed?..."

Eric had to wait a long three seconds before Scarleto said, "Agreed, best of luck in your future." Then both of them hung up.

With his phone call done, he turned his attention to the television set. The news was featuring some rerun footage of Firestone being bombarded by reporters after he returned to Whales' side following losing him in the development zone. In the footage, Firestone had declined to make any comments, got into his car, and after a few honks to break up the media mob that was practically crawling on his hood, drove to God only knew where.

"Where are you Anthony? Do you know that I know who you are? Do you know who I am yet; where I am; when we will see each other again? Do you know where your partner is?" Eric wondered aloud then laughed sickeningly.

The footage of Firestone went still then shrunk to the corner of the screen. Rebecca Whales, now seated comfortably at the anchor desk and wearing a spicy red number, then dominated the screen. She began reiterating facts about the disaster; the most recent death toll, the most recent injury count, naming the pop-up clinics where people could get treatment for minor injuries and illnesses to help keep emergency rooms manageable, and so on. Then she apologized, *again*, for her role in the fact that no was arrested yet.

As she rambled, he made one last sweep of the house, making certain he had not left so much as a finger print behind. Satisfied, he left the remainder of the rent that he owed in an envelope on the bathroom sink and the keys to the place next to that envelope as he and his landlady had agreed on over the phone the previous day.

Upon returning to the living room, he noticed that two impeccably accurate sketches of himself had replaced the frozen footage of Firestone at the corner of the screen; one sketch depicted his infectious rashes and the other depicted how he would look as a healthy man. He paused briefly, admiring Firestone's observational skills.

Bell recognized that the only time Firestone had seen him was that brief moment that he had struggled to process the fact that he had walked into a trap; that meant that those sketches were conceived from a single moment and at a considerable distance.

Bell felt confident however, despite the sketches, because he recognized that

Firestone was wasting his time because he would be in a different city before the good folks behind the tip line would find him.

Whales' continued reporting, saying, "This man is a suspected terrorist who is allegedly responsible for the Carlton Tower's destruction. He is considered armed, dangerous, and highly infectious from the Tower Toxin. If you see him, do not approach him. Instead, call the police tip line at..." Eric stopped paying attention then.

He kissed his gloved fingertips and pressed them to the screen right where her lips were. "You can stop wasting your time, darling." He said aloud smoothly, "This is good-bye *forever*." Then turned off the TV and left.

PART TWO-AFTERMATH

Chapter 8

It was now ten days since the Carlton Tower fell and despite the fact that no arrests were made, the city had improved in every other way. The hospitals now had an effective treatment for the Tower Toxin, so most people were cured overnight. The cure made it so that all of the hospitals were rapidly becoming more able to return to their normal routines. The volunteer pop-up clinics were beginning to close and the out-of-town medical staff brought in to work them began returning home; the city was starting to stand on its own again.

Whatever was left of the Carlton Tower after the devastation was demolished, the site was cleared of bodies and debris, and a temporary faux-brass monument featuring all the names of the dead was placed in the heart of the site. By now, all but nine bodies had been identified and their families had been brought in. Victim's families and caring spectators left candles, flowers, pictures, notes, and stuffed animals at the base of the monument; making what was once a site of incredible horror into a site of unity and encouragement.

The most recent and final death toll was twenty-four-thousand-sixty-three people with seven-hundred more still severely injured. Because of the quick and efficient clean-up, the first of the funerals had been and gone that morning. Lives were being rebuilt and people were moving on.

Firestone was currently driving to St. Margret's Children's Hospital. After he had been forcibly removed from the Corrocco Estate following a rather unsettling interview session with the widow Corrocco and her lawyer a few days previous, he returned to his office to find that several dry erase boards had been set up in the bullpen. The boards were labelled as 'dead', 'unaccounted for', and 'survivors' and each was covered with photos and artist's renderings of people who had been in the Carlton Tower.

Firestone had noticed then that the young woman who had lost her feet had been declared dead. He had left a bouquet of lilies in her honour at the monument when it opened, but more importantly, was the fact that a two-year-old girl by the name of Addison Smith was on the survivor's board when the rest of the Smith family had been killed nearly seventy floors above the nearest exit.

Naturally, Firestone was curious about how a child that could barely walk managed to evacuate the collapsing tower with such impressive speed without the support her family and he was going to the hospital to solve that mystery because he had learned that the things that didn't add up were the most telling where the Carlton Tower was concerned and he was eager for an encouragement infusion.

Immediately after his less-than-triumphant return from the Corrocco's, Firestone had less than five minutes to collect his thoughts before he was called up to the director's office. Now, even five days later, his ears were still ringing from their argument.

"*Firestone,*" Director Wayne Meyer shouted before Firestone could even close the door after entering, "Do you realize what a fool you have made of yourself and of this agency with that ridiculous stunt you pulled with that reporter and you chose to do so after you piss off one of the most connected women in the country? Couldn't you warn me of either?"

Director Meyer was positively fuming. His bald head and freshly shaved face were both blotchy with patches of tomato-redness and ghostly paleness. His blue eyes appeared almost purple because they were so bloodshot, his suit was ruffled, his tie simply draped over one shoulder, and he was standing hunched over his desk with his fists pushing into the desktop forcefully. His posturing reminded Firestone of a disturbed Mountain Gorilla.

"In addition, I've got political representatives from every state, country, and continent in my ear informing me how poorly we've handled the entire Carlton Tower incident. They're wondering whether or not we have any idea on where those psychos will strike next, to which I embarrassingly had to answer *'not'*. We know nothing and we have nothing *and* since you did it all hand-in-hand with the most popular reporter in the country, *everybody* knows how little we know."

Firestone opened his mouth to say something, but Meyer punched the desktop so harshly that it cracked underneath his fist and he turned his back to Firestone which effectively discouraged him from speaking. Meyer went on, "*And* now, as if all of that wasn't bad enough, you're stupid stunt made that terrorist look as speedy and as stealthy as a superhero while simultaneously making us *and* the local PD look like bumbling boneheads. *That,* that Firestone, had both national and international implications. *Everyone* now believes that the law enforcement force in this city is cripplingly unprepared to defend its citizens and its country against anything more than rogue shopping charts and blind old ladies with valid driver's licenses. There are already protests blooming in our streets and the streets of neighbouring cities and states *and...*"

Just then, Firestone's cell phone rang. Firestone removed it from his pocket and read the caller ID as he pressed 'ignore'. The call was from Angelique and Firestone was confident it could wait.

Satisfied he had his attention again when the phone went back into Firestone's pocket, Meyer resumed, only this time, he was much calmer and seated. "When they call me back, I want to be able to restore their faith in us."

Firestone's phone began to ring again, but he Meyer finish. "Let's get a handle on these bastards and ask for forgiveness later if we need to, agreed?"

"Agreed," Firestone said as he finally answered a persistent Angelique.

As soon as Firestone answered, before he could even say hello, he heard her say, "His name is Bell."

"What?" Firestone asked, grabbing Director Meyer's attention.

"I've been running that sketch you composed of that terrorist you ran down through my new internet web and we got facial recognition hits from the armed forces database, Interpol, and TSA. It seems your guy's birth name is John Murphy Bell. After a dishonourable discharge from Special Forces, he adopted the first name of Eric and he switches last names between his smuggling operations and contract killings."

"TSA has him entering our fair city under the name Eric Timothy Bell. Also, Detective Donna Sparks got back to me and confirmed that the blood sample we collected following the sting attempt matched the ID, thanks to an earlier Interpol operation that got some of this guy's DNA for us to match to."

"We have him on the ropes, we just need to put him in a cell and then he's as good as convicted."

Firestone put Angelique on speaker and had her repeat what she had just told him to a curious Director Meyer. With the director clued in on the ID, Angelique continued, "Because we now had a name and an unobstructed face to work with, I was able to use the kaleidoscope, infrared, and GPS satellite tracking from my new web as well to track his movements virtually every step of the way."

"I tracked him to an income property owned by a Mitilda Green. She's seventy-two years old and has a bad hip so she's probably not a freedom fighter, but more importantly is the fact that I followed Bell from the apartment building where you lost him back to that house."

Angelique began speaking faster and faster; mincing her words into choppy, breathy, run-on sentences. "Guys, based on phone records coming out of that house, Bell phoned his landlady minutes after he returned there. He left the house early the next morning and got into a cab that left town and I lose him after that, but his landlady showed up there less than half-an-hour after Bell leaves; she relisted it minutes after she went in, so he likely phoned to tell her that he was leaving."

"The profilers down here think that, in Bell's adrenaline-fueled haste to escape, he may have told her where he was planning on going when he made that call. If not that, my records suggest the two met frequently, so she could be our best way yet to get into Bell's head!"

Unfortunately, Firestone would never meet Ms. Green because, about an hour after Angelique's call, the planned press conference was held and an overzealous Director Meyer gave the live media audience *everything* they had thus far on Bell and his landlady Mitilda Green. Meyer also introduced a non-practical initiative named 'REDEMPTION' that essentially demanded that every lead that came into the tip line be investigated by an officer, but unfortunately, all the press conference did was spread law enforcement thin; chasing tips that lead nowhere. The conference also turned people's fear into anger and gave them a place to focus that anger; Mitilda Green.

Before any law enforcement could stop it, Mitilda was lynched by an angry mob that was convinced she was complicit in Bell's actions and escape.

Firestone was then forced to spend the next few days putting out press fires instead of tracking down Bell.

Firestone was not on the greatest terms with Director Meyer and he was on even worse terms with the press, so he needed some fresh leads.

He was hopeful that learning what happened to Addison Smith and hearing the stories from some others who were with her would give him those leads because Bell had obviously escaped similarly to how they had. He held on to that hope as he pulled up to the hospital's machine designed to dispense parking receipts.

He parked, walked in to the hospital, and found a delightful nurse named Joanna who helped him find Addison and her soon to be adopted mother right away.

When he walked into her room, she was colouring with some paper and crayons provided her. She was wearing fuzzy pink pajamas with grey kittens on them. Her blonde was messily tied into a ponytail. She smiled when he walked in and cheerfully asked, "Are you a prince?"

He laughingly said, "No, I'm a police officer. I want to ask you some questions about how you ended up here in the hospital."

"You mean when the fun place wasn't so fun anymore." She said sadly.

Firestone looked down at Addison's picture and realised that it showed her holding the hand of her adoptive mother and a family of angel up in the clouds above them. Firestone's throat felt half its size when he swallowed because he knew before she explained what it was of.

"This is my mom, my dad, and my sisters; they had to go to heaven when the fun place fell down, but they're happy that I have my new mom and she loves me lots."

Firestone smiled through some tears and told her, "Yes she does. You're a lucky girl and I'm happy that you're here. Can I ask you my questions as we colour?"

She nodded, handed him some paper and some crayons, and they talked.

After spending about half-an-hour with Addison, colouring and enjoying chocolate chip cookies and milk while sneaking in the occasional question, he learned that a 'strong, scary man that smelled funny' convinced her daddy to let him carry her out. The man she described seemed like Bell, but he could not be certain.

He was confused about why Bell would take the risk of showing himself to Addison's family and slowing himself down with Addison's weight.

Addison also described a kind of bungee jumping experience. Apparently her rescuer ninja jumped over the safety rails on certain flights of stairs and ultimately 'flew' between a Carlton Tower balcony and the roof next door. Her rescuer ultimately helped her down the emergency escape on the exterior of the safe building.

Based on the complexity of the escape, Firestone became immediately confident that her rescuer was Bell, but he still questioned Bell's motives.

He needed a clearer picture that he felt he could only get from an adult, and since thinking of her frightening experience and the loss of her family exhausted Addison, Firestone stepped out to talk to her soon to be mom, hoping she could give him more.

"She's a special girl," Firestone said quietly as he sat with Addison's adoptive mother on a built-in bench across the hall from, but still looking into Addison's room. "I'd like to hear how the two of you ended up together..."

She glanced tearfully at Addison before looking back at Firestone and explaining, "I'm a traffic enforcement officer. I was working the intersection of Beacon Avenue and King Street because the traffic lights there had been blown out by a drunk driver crashing into them the week before." The intersection she'd been working was less than two full blocks away from the Tower. In fact, Beacon Avenue turned right in to the Tower's parking lot.

She continued, "The blast actually knocked me down and left my ears ringing." Firestone raised his eyebrows, but continued to listen; this was exactly the prospective that Firestone hoped he would get from coming to this hospital.

"When I got my bearings back, I saw smoke and flames raging from the upper part of the tower, but I couldn't focus on that because many of the motorists I was guiding had gone off the road. Several pedestrians and motorists had suffered minor injuries as a result of the blast forces."

"I was a Military Medical Corpsman before I joined the police academy and got assigned to traffic, so my training kicked in. I ran back up a few blocks and stopped traffic at a safe distance. While I blocked traffic, I used my radio to call in the blast and the traffic related injuries surrounding it."

"With the intersection secured and help arriving quickly, I used my basic medical training to help the injured motorists and pedestrians before going to the tower area and doing the best that I could there." She swallowed hard and wiped her tears away with her fingers, "There was just so much destruction, so many injuries, and so much panic." Firestone nodded comfortably, remembering his own horrifying experience at the scene. He was there when the scene was mostly sorted and still it was hard for him to take.

He hesitated to imagine what it would've been like being there without support which was when this saint of a woman was putting her own fears and injuries aside to help the stricken strangers at the scene.

"As more and more qualified professionals arrived," she went on, "I took a step back and started controlling the looky-loos. When I was working the crime scene line, that John Bell guy from the news brought Addison to me." She confirmed his suspicion, but Bell's actions still confused him.

Firestone's face twisted with his confusion as the same unanswered questions filled his mind. The woman misinterpreted his expression and immediately went on the defensive, "I promise you that there was nothing about him that suggested he was a terrorist. In fact, he sold himself to me as a distressed guy whose girlfriend was missing in the panic. As things settled, I did notice that no one could account for him, but I mistakenly assumed that he'd found his missing girlfriend and was at the hospital with her or something and at the time I had Addison in my arms and we needed some medical care of our own."

"When the first sketch came out, it didn't even register with me that was him and when the later news came out, with the clearer likeness of him included, it was followed by the news that another person who had a passing connection to him was lynched; I had to think of Addison." Firestone nodded and thanked her for her help and service. When they parted, she went back to Addison's side, leaving Firestone to ponder his thoughts alone on the bench for a few moments.

As Firestone pondered, Addison's nurse reappeared with a young boy clinging to her hip. He looked to be about twelve-years-old, his left arm was in sling, and his head was bandaged right down over his left eye. Under his free arm, he carried a toy drone and a high-tech remote for it. "Mr. Firestone, Joey here has something we think you should see..." the nurse explained.

"Are you a police officer?" The boy asked as he began to excitedly pull away from Joanna's side.

"I'm a Federal Agent actually," Firestone answered with a smile, "C'mon, show me what you've got Joey."

Joey nodded and set himself up on the bench next to Firestone. Once he was settled, he turned his toy's remote on. It was then that Firestone realized that the drone had a video function with footage still on it from inside the Carlton Tower!

It looked like the footage had been shot while the drone hovered and wavered between the second and third levels of the mall. "I'm not so sure because my eyes aren't really good anymore, but isn't that the guy from the TV?" Joey pointed to a fast moving figure his drone struggled to follow as he crossed the mall and entered the elevator. The footage was relatively low quality and was quite distant, but the figure's height, build, and clearly-goal-driven movements were definitely accurate for Bell.

Along the way, the figure occasionally changed clothes and checked his phone, but through it all he carried the same bag; it probably contained the restaurant bomb.

Joey was more than happy to hand over the remote so that the footage could be processed professionally by the Cyber Unit and for his trouble, Firestone pinned a mini-badge pin to his hospital pajamas which clearly made Joey's day.

Firestone had just stood up to leave when he noticed a doctor standing with a tired and teary woman. Their conversation was intense, so he decided not to interrupt them by passing by. He sat down again, but he could not help overhearing.

"Unfortunately Liam was the only one we could save," The doctor said glumly. The woman rocked back and forth; her body contracted with silent sobs. The doctor grabbed her shoulder.

She calmed herself relatively quickly and asked, "Can I see him?"

"No," The doctor said hesitantly. It was clear he was sympathetic, but he still had to tell her, "Unfortunately, he hasn't regained consciousness as quickly as we were expecting. Several of Liam's vertebra and the corresponding nerve packets were critically damaged by the force of the blast. The full extent of the damage and how permanent it is can only be determined in time and with consciousness, but Liam's slowness to regain consciousness could indicate a more serious problem. He could have damage higher up on the spine and there could be brain damage. We need to keep the room clear in case he takes a turn for the worst and we to operate, but we *will* do everything we can and we will keep you posted." The doctor nodded at her, urging a response while also allowing him to check her for signs of shock and hysteria.

She nodded then slumped down on a bench the width of a doorway away from where Firestone was seated. The doctor became agitated. He explained, "I hate to leave you like this, but I have patients that need me..."

The woman waved the doctor off without looking him in the eyes again saying, "Of course, go."

The doctor left quickly. Seeing her alone didn't seem right to Firestone, so he went over and sat with her. She had a few minor wound, but even despite them, she was a stunningly beautiful brunette with exotic features that told Firestone she was middle-eastern; Israeli maybe.

They sat in silence for a moment while he found the right words. He introduced himself casually while utilizing hesitant, but appropriate hand gestures, "I'm special Agent

Anthony Firestone; I'm the Special Agent in charge of the Carlton Tower attack and I'm sorry for your suffering." She nodded appreciatively. Firestone continued, "Was Liam a tower employee?"

She shook her head and took a chunk of *something* off her belt and handed it to Firestone. To Firestone's disbelief, the thing she handed him was a deformed and scuffed detective's badge. Her voice was exotic and silky. "I'm Detective Donna Sparks out of the twenty-third precinct." Firestone recognized her name. She was the Detective responsible for handling the local police's portion of the Carlton Tower investigation. According to Angelique, she was also the person that confirmed Angelique's ID of Bell using the blood sample that was collected following the blown sting meant to bring Bell to justice.

"It's a pleasure putting a face to your name." He said engaging her in an awkward and small handshake. "Our Cyber Technologist is your biggest fan, I think."

She smiled and awkwardly chuckled as she wiped some tears from her eyes. She spoke softly, letting him see her face for the first time since he sat down as she took her badge back from him, "Liam was my partner and one of his confidential informants brought our attention to an African migrant he thought was a meth cook. The kid was occupying an abandoned warehouse near the Carlton Tower and was approaching local low-level drug dealers and getting information from them on underground chemical suppliers so he could buy chemicals in bulk without raising red flags."

Firestone found himself hanging on her every word. When he sat down, had expected to be comforting a soon-to-be widow, but instead he found himself discussing details he didn't know about the case. He listened intently as she went into more interesting detail, "He must have found what wanted because the CI told us he saw the kid moving bulk bags of chemicals and other equipment like gallon pales and a trashy claw-foot tub into the broken-down abandoned warehouse that is a common junky and squatter hub."

She swallowed and caught her breath, but then continued, "We didn't jump on the lead because, unfortunately, small time drug cooks tend to be low on the priority list when we're busy looking for rapists and murderers, but after about a week, we noticed that no new drugs were hitting the streets. We began to wonder what the kid was doing, so we put a surveillance team on him."

"The surveillance team came back with intel that the kid bought blasting caps and electrical cord. He also had mystery crates: contents unknown. We decided that was too suspicious so we arranged to raid his warehouse."

She started to tear up again. She swallowed and continued to explain, "Liam and I, accompanied by our regular S.W.A.T team and some techies from the bomb squad, clustered outside the warehouse in a standard raid formation, but just as we were about to breach, The Carlton Tower blew. Liam and I put two-and-two together and decided the kid was likely the bomber, so we..."

She sobbed, but caught herself and finished, "We breached, not knowing there were trip-wires blockading the doors." As she spoke, Firestone remembered the second blast he swore he heard as the dust cloud from the Carlton Tower swept over him; that second blast must have been the warehouse Donna was talking about.

As much as he wanted to interject, he didn't speak up and share this with her; he simply let her continue, "Liam and I were lined up behind the tactical specialists. We were thrown back by the blast and cut by shrapnel, but we hardly caught the worst of it; or at least, I thought we were ok until Liam passed out while he was treating my wounds..." She brushed her hair behind her ear, allowing Firestone to see that her ear was heavily bandaged and that there were several deep cuts jutting out from the bandaging. Especially considering that they had already had ten days to heal, there was no doubt that Donna's injuries were much worse than he first thought.

"I had a bad concussion. I was too dizzy to do anything, but call in the incident as I sat by the car, but Liam pushed himself to go and check for other survivors; he found none and fell at my feet."

"Because of the Tower blowing up also, the paramedics took too long to find us. There was nothing they could due for the rest of our team and Liam only got worse."

"We knew the S.W.A.T and bomb squad guys very well. They were like family to us..." She stood up and began to pace in a stressed manner as her eyes met Firestone's briefly.

Firestone nodded understandingly, "I'm so sorry; I lost friends in the disaster, but I did not experience their losses so closely. Have you spoken to anyone; have taken time to process everything?"

She nodded, appreciating the condolences and concern, but simply said, "I'm working on it."

Her response did not sufficiently suggest to Firestone that she was allowing herself to grieve properly which put her mental state and competence as an investigator in question, but he felt he had no right to press the issue, so he reverted back to the case. "Are you telling me you have insider access on the suspected Carlton Tower bomber?"

Donna starred him down. She seemed almost manic as she said, "Yes. If you accompany me back to my precinct, I will give you everything."

Firestone was slightly caught off guard, but he nodded and followed her back to the twenty-third precinct by car.

Chapter 9

The twenty-third precinct was famous at the federal level for having the highest successful conviction rate in the city, but today it more closely resembled an average school gym immediately after hurricane Katrina in New Orleans.

As Firestone entered the front doors to the precinct, his senses were immediately overwhelmed. Going into the precinct, there was a fifteen-step staircase leading up to the front office and a small elevator to the left of the stairs. There were lines of people crowding both the stairs and the elevator.

Many of the people were loaded down with camping gear. Those people were clearly unwashed and several of them had minor injuries such as deep cuts and severe bruising; they smelled like sweat and infection. Firestone was struck by the fact that he recognized many of their faces from the boards in his own bullpen. They were survivors from the Carlton Tower when it blew.

Other people in the crowds looked a lot cleaner and healthier, but they were loaded down with enough paperwork to take up a week for ten people. Many were struggling unsuccessfully to find seats in the rapidly filling lobby and many of them settled uncomfortably on the steps.

Still, Sparks and Firestone managed to weave through the crowds and badged their way passed the overwhelmed front office staff who were hopelessly trying give order and direction to the desperate mob.

As they moved, they overheard more than one person ask if they could sleep in a cell as their homes were deemed inhabitable because of the dust and debris from the blast sites, leaving them with nowhere else to go. Others were outraged because they were victims of 'every day crimes', but because law enforcement was spread so thin, no one had responded.

Firestone felt a sudden pain in his chest; he was really bothered by all of the suffering he had seen over the past two weeks and he wished he could do more to resolve it, but ultimately, he felt the best way to help everyone was to solve this case so that the city could rebuild without living with the fear of the group attacking again. They continued through the doorway and into the heart of the precinct where Firestone discovered it was devastated in a different fashion.

While the front office was suffocated by people, the bullpen was more like a graveyard. Just over half of the desks in the bullpen were virtually empty aside from framed photos nested in small flowered wreaths; the desks were obviously shrines to the officers that once sat in them. The phones and computers on the emptied desks had been temporarily disconnected which cut the noise that a trained officer like Firestone had grown accustomed to hearing; the lack of this noise created an eerie and depressing environment.

Donna's desk was almost square in the center of the bullpen area. It was clearly loaded down with case files, forensic reports, jotted phone messages, and mail; some of the mail was open and some wasn't. Although it was clearly loaded down, her desk was clearly sorted and organized. Even the roughly jotted phone messages that were skewered by a small and obscure desk toy seemed somehow colour-coded. There was also a wide-square calendar filled to the edges with activities; some were personal, most were work related, and all were timed to within fifteen minutes for starts and finishes. Firestone was both impressed and jealous of her insane organizational skills.

Her organizational skills also made Firestone's time at the twenty-third pass quickly. She grabbed up and handed him all the information he needed in less than two seconds. As she handed him the paperwork, she told him, "This is the original copy of *everything* we have." She surprised Firestone by flipping open the thickest file and explaining, "This is the information on Liam's informant. It has his full name, cell number, and the three most likely places that he can be found."

She flipped those pages and went on, "This is everything we had on the warehouse that was the bombers workshop. It includes information on the former owners, workmen, squatters, and anyone else that may have had keys or gained entry and the most updated floor plan."

"The rest of this is our report on the investigation. It includes all of the information we have on the suspect; the CI's formal statement, the surveillance package, and my incident report of the breach."

She took a second to breathe and Firestone could tell she was briefly revisiting the incident that killed her team, but she carried herself through it. She closed the thickest file and opened the next thickest one, saying, "Then you have the crime scene photos. You'll notice that some photos have attached notes that reference reports that relate to them."

"You'll see as you read into the reports more closely that most of the DNA evidence is skewed because the force of the blast threw the DNA of my boys *everywhere*. Not to mention, there is a lot of blood, urine, and half-eaten food evidence from the homeless and junky population helping to call whatever other evidence remains into question. Also, none of the fingerprints we recovered matched the man our informant described, but the surveillance team tied our guy to this green Oldsmobile, this black suburban, and this silver SUV. Given the suspected Carlton Tower connection we did our research. Ms. Marceau confirmed that the black suburban pulled into the underground parking structure of the Tower about eight hours before the blast, so it is likely our bomb car; the bomb that destroyed the foundation."

"It's difficult to tell," Donna said, slowly getting more excited, "But this blurry dark figure in the driver's seat is more than likely our African American suspect." Firestone nodded in agreement.

Donna continued, "Unfortunately, Ms. Marceau couldn't confirm his identity, but according to the DMV the suburban and the SUV were both purchased close together about four months ago and our informant indicated this guy moved into the area six months ago. I'm thinking the Oldsmobile is his personal vehicle and he bought the SUV and suburban for the job and if the suburban is the bomb car..."

"Then the SUV is likely the group's getaway car..." Firestone interjected equally as excited.

"Yes!" Donna cheered. It was clear that both of them were missing the collaborative thinking that they got from working with their partners' and that void being filled created sparks between them. They found themselves interlocked in a stare that was better suited for a perfume commercial than a work stricken police precinct. They realized the position they were in and turned away awkwardly.

Donna spoke up again, "There's one more thing you should know Firestone..."

"Yes what?" He asked, pivoting on his heels.

"When Liam and I first began to suspect terrorism, we brought in our Captain and the three of us sat for a conference call with your agency." Firestone raised his eyebrows as Donna continued, "A special agent Clara Fife took a copy of virtually everything you've got now and she said she'd quote, 'I'll handle it.'"

They both starred at each other, wide-eyed and white-faced. Donna nodded because she knew by his expression that Firestone understood the heavy implications of what she was telling him.

The fact that Donna and her people had alerted the FBI to a suspected terrorist near the Carlton Tower told Firestone that one of three things had happened. One, someone in his agency could have prevented the Carlton Tower tragedy, but they dropped the ball and were they continuing to obstruct justice by not admitting their mistake. If this was the case, the agent in question deserved to be fired.

Two, someone inside his agency was assisting the terrorists and deliberately obstructing the investigation by convincing the authorities that the case was being handled. If this was the case, the agent needed to be arrested.

Three, someone from outside his agency had managed to insert themselves into it and take control of the investigation. If this was case, he needed to make an arrest and shore up the security breach that allowed them to get that close in the first place.

He had a lot on his mind as he drove back to his office.

Chapter 10

Firestone was fairly certain he knew all of the female staff in the office, but he had never heard of an Agent Clara Fife. After a brief discussion with Director Meyers who then called in a few favors with a well respected and politically connected judge, Firestone managed to get approval to review the entire agency's employee roster as well as all of the phone records for the twenty-third precinct in an effort to pin down who Donna and her team had reported to.

Firestone enlisted Angelique's help to comb through the massive amounts of names and numbers and, as Firestone suspected, there were no Clara Fifes on the roster, so their search was not easy.

Finally, after hours of searching Angelique announced, "There's our buried treasure!" as she highlighted a phone call from the precinct to the FBI's lead International Call Center.

"For what time?" Firestone asked. He intended to take the direct route through the piles of calls emanating from his FBI office and neighbouring ones.

"4:30 pm five Thursday's ago," Angelique explained gently.

Firestone flipped and skimmed with his finger to the slice of the page where the call should have been. "I see the call made it to the Call Center and," Firestone swallowed hard as he realized a worst case scenario had come true, "was forwarded here…"

"Whose extension did the call come in to?" Angelique asked as she prepared her computer to refine and speed the search.

"429-271" 429 directed the call to the Organized Crime Unit 271 went to specific agent's phone.

Firestone slammed his fist on Angelique's desk and pivoted again on his heels in frustration. 271 was an extension that belonged to an agent who had died years earlier. The desk had sat empty for those years which meant the person who had answered the call could have been anyone.

"Lucky for you," Angelique said in a temperamental way that showed her disappointment in Firestone attitude, "I anticipated that something like this might happen, so I ordered the surveillance footage for the time period we're researching. We can skim through it to the time of the call, isolate the desk the call came in on, and then enhance the image of whoever answers the phone and then I can ID her."

An exasperated Firestone reluctantly consented to continuing and it was good he did because Angelique's plan worked perfectly. The enhanced image of a beautiful faced brunette matched the ID of a recent transfer agent by the name of Claudia Fife, but Donna and her team claimed they'd spoken to someone named Clara, not Claudia. Both Angelique and Firestone attributed the discrepancy in the names to the fact that the woman's identity was likely false and she bungled up the fake name that she was unfamiliar with. Angelique continued to research into who that woman really was while Firestone ran up to the Organized Crime Unit in an effort to find and arrest her.

When he reached organized crime's bullpen, he saw a young temp packing up Claudia Fife's desk. He knew the temp well, so he wasn't suspicious of her, but he still needed the evidence she was collecting. "Hey Karen, stop! Hand me that box, please!"

She spun around to face him. She was clearly startled, "Of course Tony, here." She handed him the box and stepped away from the still-loaded desk. He calmed briefly and nodded appreciatively, but he tensed up again when she asked, "What's going on?"

He was tense because he was uncertain of the extent of Claudia Fife's guilt and was nervous that there may be others working with her. He was hesitant to let unsubstantiated rumors leak out because they could be completely wrong and could potentially ruin the life of a good person that made a mistake. It could also alert the terrorists to how close the investigation was getting. Finally, he said, "New evidence has come to light that suggests she may know more about what happened to the Carlton Tower than the rest of us do. I need to talk her about it. Do you know where I can find her?"

After a moment to let her shock to wear off, Karen slumped sadly and said, "She's dead, Tony."

Chapter 11

Getting from the Organized Crime Unit down to the morgue was a blur for Firestone, but he somehow found himself standing over the freshly-autopsied body of Delia Horsoff. Delia Horsoff was a well-known member of several Ukrainian extremist groups; she was also the not-so-federal-agent named Claudia Fife. Angelique was able to confirm her identity by running what information they did know about her through her new cyber web.

Her prints and DNA from the morgue confirmed the match.

Delia Horsoff, in addition to being a known terrorist in the Ukraine, was also a Russian-military-trained assassin and British-educated computer expert that was an asset to every terrorist group that encountered her. However the variety of groups she was associated with suggested to Firestone that she was motivated more by money and fame than by ideology, which made the apparent motivation behind the Carlton Tower disaster even more suspect for Firestone.

In his opinion, a group that no one had heard about coming out of the blue with one of the biggest attacks in history didn't sit right with him. There were people in his agency and others that were paid hundreds of thousands of dollars a year to flag any suspicious individual or group, even if they were just kids being a little too insensitive on social media. The group that attacked the Carlton Tower seemed thrown together over night and that feeling seemed to be supported by the difficult to-pin-down character profiles of Bell and Horsoff. Everything Firestone learned made the whole disaster seem *staged*, but he couldn't prove why he felt that way.

Suddenly, the voice of Doctor Richard Kane pulled Firestone back to reality, "So T-bone, what's your interest in this one?"

Richard's favorite meal was a tie-for-first-place between a fully-loaded hot dog from the cart down the block from the morgue and fish and chips with imported beer from the restaurant near his home. His poor meal choices showed. Richard was forty-seven; he had slowly greying red hair and blood-shot black eyes. He had an unhealthy and almost corpse-like bluish hue to his skin and nails and although he only stood five-foot-eight-inches, he weighed three-hundred-ninety pounds. He also kept himself almost unprofessionally scruffy.

Today, Doctor Richard Kane looked worse than usual. His thinning hair looked unwashed and was sloppily combed into an out-of-style comb-over. His facial scruff was bushier than usual and he seemed exhausted, probably from the sixteen to eighteen hours days he had steadily put in since the blast had occurred. His workload had increased to an unrealistic level with the massive loss of life from the Tower's collapse. Bodies filled the morgue beyond capacity. Bodies filled the neighbouring hallways and caused temporary morgues made from special event tents to be set up in the surrounding parking lot area. Some of Kane's regular staff had also left to work in hospitals and clinics to assist the living instead of the dead which increased his workload even more. A few other pathologists and their staff had been brought in to assist, but they brought their regular workload with them, so they barely helped.

Firestone fluffed his hair in a frustrated fashion as he explained, "Angelique from Cyber and I have uncovered some evidence that suggests this woman was one of the terrorists responsible for this disaster…"

Richard looked down at her and nodded, saying, "That makes sense. This one and her three-month-old son were found dead in her hotel room four days post blast.

Their official cause of death is 'impact injuries from the blast and severe toxin infection'. The two causes are virtually indistinguishable from each other and in my opinion as far as what actually caused their deaths. Someone who wasn't afraid of being arrested should have and would have gotten herself and her child to the hospital instead of going back to a hotel room."

"Is it possible she simply assumed she and her son were fine? No one knew there was a threatening toxin until about seven hours into the rescue mission. By then, thousands of shoppers and whatnot had already evacuated the building and many had left the scene," Firestone questioned.

Kane was shaking his head, even before Firestone had finished speaking. Kane rolled her over and removed the sheet that covered her. This gave Firestone a good view of her badly scorched and scarred back. Kane explained, "She was so close to the restaurant bomb that she was burned by the heat of the explosion itself. These stab-wound-like scars you see are pieces of restaurant furnishings like chairs, tables, and dishes that were reduced to shards and weaponized by the force of the explosion. She was then thrown by the explosion's shock wave down approximately three flights of stairs."

He went on into sickening detail, "Both of her legs were broken in multiple places and the muscles and main arteries in them were damaged by the heat and shrapnel. Her pelvis was shattered and disconnected from her spine. She broke all of her ribs, dislocated both shoulders, broke virtually every bone in her left hand, broke three fingers on the right, and..." Kane used his fingers to gently move her hair from a gaping hole in her head so that Firestone could see her clearly bruised brain through. "She basically irreparably damaged her skull and brain."

Kane straightened her scalp and hair back over the wound, rolled her back over, and covered her up again, "She was losing so much blood and likely in so much pain that I'm certain it was no accident she ended up in her hotel room."

"I know for a fact that she couldn't have gotten from the Tower back to her hotel on her own with her injuries either. She definitely needed help and I suspect she got it from her boyfriend."

"And you're basing your belief that she had a boyfriend based on the fact that she had a son?" Firestone asked; his curiosity was peeked because Richard, although he looked to be on the fringe homelessness, was famous for never making statements that he couldn't support with tangible science.

Richard Kane nodded, "and because of the fax Angelique sent down for you an hour ago." Kane then led Firestone to his small office space. As a converted and cramped janitor's closet, Kane's office was the only space not occupied by bodies, but it was a temporary home for all of the mortuary paperwork and the storage room for the clothing and other personal effects that came with all of the bodies. The men had to step around large carts filled with labelled paper bags containing the personal effects of victims in the morgue as they worked their way to Richard's brutally overloaded desk.

Kane shuffled through the piles upon piles of paperwork on the desk. He was clearly frustrated and grumbling to himself as he did, but after about five minutes, he found what he was looking for. He held out a ten-or-so page document to Firestone.

Firestone took it and read that it was a DNA Type Form for Horsoff's son. It confirmed that she was his mother and that his father was another wanted assassin from Korea. Firestone flipped the page to find that Angelique had summarized the reports from several agencies as they tracked the Korean assassin's movements throughout the world.

    Kin Luk first came on the international radar when he assassinated a Korean diplomat during secret military negotiations with the Russians in Russia. Prior to the assassination Luk was a high ranking government security officer. Because of his position, Luk was privy to thousands of North Korean secrets as well as a few secrets from countries that the diplomat Luk was pretending to protect had visited. The CIA had foolishly suspected that they could convince Luk to sell them those secrets, so they moved him from Russia to Britain in a clandestine mission that quickly went bad and resulted in the deaths of all agents involved as soon they reached British soil.

Angelique suspected that Luk and Horsoff met in Britain because the next attack for which Luk was credited was the destruction of a British Aircraft Carrier. Luk was part of a five person team and, although the other two men and two women on his strike team were never officially identified, a description of one of the women matched Horsoff to a tee.

Also, Horsoff abandoned the British University she had been attending as well as her pending contract with the Russian military at around the same time as the Aircraft Carrier strike.

Horsoff reappeared thirteen months later in Spain having had her baby. She put Kin Luk's real name for the father on the child's birth certificate and although Horsoff was living under the name Sophia Luk then, she put Delia Luk on the certificate as well. That told Firestone that Kin and Delia must have gotten married or were at least seriously pretending to be. Either way, the baby's birth blew their cover and caused every agency with international outreach to take siege on the small Spanish town they were calling home.

Obviously Horsoff and Luk escaped being arrested that day, but her blowing his cover likely ended the romance between them because Luk and Horsoff were only scene cotenants apart in the time between the baby's birth and the Carlton Tower attack, approximately six months later.

Angelique's report also ended with airport surveillance of Luk entering the city arm-and-arm with a young Asian woman.

That suggested to Firestone that there was likely yet another player in this game. The key to finally making an arrest or two in this case was finding Kin Luk and his young Asian companion. With another flip to the final page of Angelique's report, he felt he could do just that because there was picture of the loving couple scampering into a low-rate motel near the airport.

Chapter 12

Within the hour; Firestone, Detective Donna Sparks, and a small cluster of four other officers from a precinct whose jurisdiction the motel fell under entered the lobby holding their badges up. Firestone had a picture of Luk and his feminine companion in hand and slid it across the desk to the attendant, but before Firestone could ask about them, the attendant caught everyone off guard by saying, "Well, it's about time you've come."

All of the officers looked at each other briefly, confused. Firestone asked, "I'm sorry?"

"We called about half an hour ago," the infuriated desk clerk explained, "We heard a gunshot from room 213. I rented that out personally to this guy too." The clerk handed the photo of Luk and his lover back to Firestone as he grabbed up his master key from the shelf just below the desk top.

The clerk then led the group of officers to room 213's door and placed the key in the lock. He waited for the officers to get into breaching formation and he nodded to Firestone, who was aligned to be first through the door, before he turned the key which unlocked the door and finally, he stepped away quickly. The clerk was clearly no stranger to police procedure which was no surprise at a motel of this caliber.

Still, Firestone and his team entered loudly and prepared for the worst. This was unnecessary. As the officers fanned out into the room, they all saw the same gory scene; a dead Kin Luk sprawled out on a blood covered made bed.

Forensics would still have to do a proper analysis, but all of the officers agreed it looked like suicide. There was a small hole in his right temple and the gun was still caressed loosely in his right hand and there was a suicide note on the dresser.

The note was propped up against an expensive-looking silver picture frame that was embossed with artistically carved leaves. Firestone photographed the picture and the note as they sat with a small camera he kept clipped to his utility belt. With the picture taken, Firestone scooped up the frame in his gloved hand to study the photo more closely.

The picture within the fancy frame was of Luk and his unidentified female companion. She was hugging him from behind and they both looked very happy. The picture was too tight in on their faces for Firestone to discern where or when the photo was taken and for a brief moment, he saw his face in place Luk's and Leah's in place of the woman's.

He returned the picture to its place on the dresser and read the relatively lengthy suicide note.

To whoever may find this,

After years of tragic mistakes, romantic and otherwise, I thought I found everything I wanted and needed in Jeanine Sing. She was smart, beautiful, artistic, and SO young. She was strong physically and emotionally and she had lived a similar life to mine.

She understood what I did and why. She understood why it was important to live a quieter and smaller life...

Then the note's tone changed aggressively.

It was supposed to be our final score, we were going to make a lot of money and then disappear forever to some sandy, sunny beach.

I didn't expect to see Delia and our son on the job, but I accepted she was a good fit for our team and our son was strong cover.

We all recognized there would be risks, but Bell made it sound manageable; he lied. I had to handle too many men to watch their backs.

I had finished clearing my room just in time to see Jeanine get shot and fall. Bell dropped the bomb beside her like she was trash. What if she was alive and died knowing she was helpless to what was coming?

In that moment, I realized what a ruthless and emotionless bastard Bell really was. I also realized how worthless any money would be without Jeanine so I tried to chase Bell down as we blended in to the frantic crowds of innocent people. I obviously didn't catch him and because I was chasing Bell instead of helping Delia, our son did not make it out of the tower alive. I went back and brought him to

Delia's room anyway because they deserved to be laid to rest together.

Once we made it back to her hotel, I realized how much I missed her. I realized that I may have been fooling myself with my belief in how happy I was with Jeanine. I felt I was using Jeanine to bury the guilt that I felt from leaving Delia because she was foolish in letting our son's birth cause a scent trail which federal agents used to nearly catch us.

I was disappointed and ran, but my love for Delia and our son never faded. I came to that realization just in time to have Delia die in my arms.

I lost Delia, I lost Jeanine, and I lost my son. I'm wanted by every law enforcement agency in every country and I have no resources left that I could use to start over and make a life for myself even if I wanted to.

The only thing that would be awaiting me now is a slow, painful death in a prison cell thanks to that damned toxin. I don't have the strength to go on anymore. For whatever it's worth, I'm sorry.

As my last act, I want to ensure Bell gets put down like the rabid dog that he is; I hope this helps.

Stapled to the nearly three-full-page suicide note was a step-by-step outline of the whole Carlton Tower attack. It featured a printout of the underground website and corresponding chat room the team met on, emails between the entire team that outlined what each member was responsible for and even what they should wear for their jobs.

Luk also threw in the copies of the Carlton Tower specifications. The specs included designs for where the offices were, where the security cameras were, where the alarms were, and where all of the maintenance shutoffs were. Using the provided specs, this team could have planted their explosives next to a gas line or a fuse box. If they had done that, they would have caused significantly more damage. Why didn't they go for that? The answer to that question was not included in Luk's package.

Later, Director Meyers hosted another press conference in which Firestone got to tell the world that three of the five terrorists responsible for the Carlton Tower disaster had been located and were deceased. After Firestone had finished his comforting and inspiring speech, Meyers took over and boldly suggested that the terrorists' earlier threat of more attacks was a bluff. He called the Brotherhood for a Pure America nothing but gutless brutes with too much time on their hands and not enough brains to be worth worrying about. His comments were brutal and endless. Firestone worried that they would come back around to bite them, but with three of five terrorist neutralized and his agency rapidly closing in on the other two, he felt satisfied with putting that out of his mind temporarily as he went home for some much needed rest.

As Firestone drove home from the auditorium where the press conference was held, he couldn't shake the feeling that he was missing something important that was right in front of him. This feeling gained strength as Firestone acknowledged the fact that something about the whole Carlton Tower scenario felt familiar to him; he couldn't place either feeling though and was left grinding his teeth and causing his knuckles to turn white from his grip on the steering wheel as he drove.

Chapter 13

Pinpricks of rain tapped his windows and rooftop as Firestone settled into his fourth story apartment much later that evening. Normally, Firestone stewed over his dislike for his landlord-and-lady-controlled purple and red walled bedroom, but today that eye scoring, feminine room looked like a paradise island retreat. He dropped his gear, stripped off his suit, and collapsed on his bed without bothering to crawl under the covers or even to align his head with the pillow.

As he slept, he began to dream. In his dream, he was in an off-white, relaxing room, nestled comfortably into a luxurious bed. Just as he was about to drift off into another dream, Leah stepped in wearing sexy black lingerie she climbed on to him, sighed, and smiled. She asked, "What's going on Tony?"

He raised his eyebrows, surprised that they were talking instead of loving, "You tell me," he laughed.

"Why haven't you made an arrest yet?" Leah asked.

"Well, so far, everyone we've been able to catch up with has already died. As for Bell, I'm working it."

"Tony," Leah said softly, "Are you struggling because I'm not there with you?"

Firestone softened and cupped Leah's face in his hands, "I'd be lying if I said that wasn't part of it. You inspire me, focus me, and help me in so many more ways that I have grown to depend on over the years, but I want the bastards responsible for what happened to the tower; I really do, but I just can't figure them out."

Touched, Leah said, "Oh Tony, you should know that whatever happens and whether you like it or not, I am always with you. Now that you know something is wrong, let's make it right."

"I thought we just made it right; I miss you and that is affecting my work. I've acknowledged that and promise I will work on it moving forward. Can we have sex now?"

Leah laughed, "Slow down there, tiger; we're almost there, but you know that something is wrong. Let's pin down what that is, then it's playtime."

"Very well," Firestone said with a laugh. He was doing a poor job of pretending to be defeated. "The biggest thing that has been bothering me is, Bell is clearly a monster; he killed hundreds of innocent men women and children so why did Bell save Addison Smith?"

"That's an easy answer," Leah said. "Addison is simply a distraction, and she's a good one at that. After all, she distracted that heroic traffic officer from detaining Bell and caused you to spend an entire afternoon learning about her instead of hunting Bell."

"You're right, aren't you?" Firestone asked

"Yes, so what else are you questioning?" An intrigued Leah asked.

"I don't think any of them are terrorists. They strike me more as hired muscle, but why would anyone hire a kill-squad to destroy the Carlton Tower?"

"The most logical reason would be to kill someone..." Leah said thoughtfully.

"Ok, but to do what Bell did took risk, planning, and help. His services were so professional that they clearly were very expensive, so who would be rich enough to afford him and passionate enough to actually take that risk in hiring him. More importantly, who would be worth so much effort to kill?"

All of sudden, all of the pieces clicked together in Firestone's mind, "I know the answer to both!" He got up and began to dress.

Leah swung her feet over the edge of the bed and, while laughing said, "Tony, I'm glad you know who to arrest, but you're going to have to wake up to do it."

"Oh yeah right," he gave her a peck on the lips and said, "I'll see you in the real world." She nodded and, as she did, she and the rest of the dream room melted into a white light. After being nearly blinded by that light, he awoke.

The soft rhythm of the pinpricks of rain he had heard while falling asleep had evolved into a fully-powered thunderstorm, complete with power-flickering lightening strikes and structure-shaking thunder; Firestone did not care.

He prepared himself a balanced pork chop dinner, complete with mashed potatoes and carrots. He then jumped into a hot shower. Once he finished eating and showering, he stepped into a clean and freshly pressed grey suit, and completed all of his grooming rituals.

As he studied his considerably improved appearance in the mirror he was relieved to see that he had regained his devilishly handsome and confident demur because he would need it in the hours ahead.

He pulled on a black jacket for rain protection and as he got into his car and drove away, watching his apartment building shrink in his rear-view mirror, he thought about how he was not coming back there until he had closed the Carlton Tower case. He knew he was going into battle, but after his good meal, good sleep, and good shower; he felt ready to win it.

PART THREE-ANOTHER STORM

Chapter 14

The late hour and the rain caused some delays, but about four hours after his empowering dream, an eager Firestone sat across an interrogation table from a fatigued and weepy Elise Corrocco and a cranky counsellor Marc Perkins.

The dazed widow Corrocco surveyed her surroundings. Firestone could see her taking note of the scarred dark metal table almost pressing against her, the uncomfortable and matching metal chairs they were all sitting on, and the room's dated textured brownish-yellow tiled walls. Halfway up the wall to her right was the dark and menacing two-way mirror. She rubbed the soles of her feet on the dark-brown tiled floor, tapped the single dated hanging lamp offering pour light over head with her fingertips, and then stared at the bulky surveillance camera running in the right corner in front of her. Finally she said, "This room is a lot less friendly than my living room."

An irate Perkins growled, "Don't say anything else, Elise. Firestone here clearly wants to retire early and he'll get his wish once our friends in the oval office tell his director about his grasping at straws."

Firestone was unfazed, he stared coldly at the widow Corrocco before opening the thick Carlton Tower Disaster File and unloaded more than a dozen photos of victims from the disaster. The photos were a sickening variety of men, women, and children of all races, ages, and walks of life. He aligned each crime scene photo with a family photo of the same person which forced Ms. Corrocco and Perkins to acknowledge the devastation on a deeply emotional *and human* level.

After giving them a minute to ensure his point sunk in, Firestone pointed to individual people in the photos, saying, "This woman will never get to see her twelve-year-old daughter, graduate high school, graduate college, get married, or have kids of her own because her daughter is dead now."

"This man was confirming a sponsorship deal at a business in the tower to be an Olympic Runner. The blast cost him his legs and his career."

"This man will never hug his son again because the blast cost him his arms."

"This woman will never see how her fiancé looks in his wedding tux because a head injury she sustained escaping the blast left her blind. I could go on and on, but I'll save you the misery. Hopefully you two will be willing tell the truth and end this suffering quickly."

"What are you suggesting?" A slightly less confident Perkins asked.

"I'm not suggesting anything," Firestone shot back as he collected the photos and returned them to the file. "I'm telling you what I *know*."

Firestone elaborated, "Elise's grandfather founded the Tower nearly two-hundred years ago. He put his family name, Carlton, on the tower then and made it the family's mission to make every shopper and business person in it feel like part of the family." Elise Corrocco nodded and Firestone knew he had her helplessly hooked.

He went on, "Since it was founded, the Carlton Tower has always been more about its people than its bottom line," Elise kept nodding so Firestone continued, "That is, until you married Martin Corrocco."

Elise froze, but the recognition on her face told him that he was thinking correctly. He continued, but he softened. He even reached out and stroked her hand as he spoke, "Martin was a world famous corporate head hunter before he married you. He bought and sold, compacted and expanded, and reshaped various businesses before he married you and took over the tower from you after you married. He *completely* took over didn't he?" It took a few long seconds, but eventually she gave in and gave him another nod.

"His tastes are different from yours; that's evident from your living room. It's filled with warm colours and low maintenance furnishings, but it is also scarred with ridiculously priced and tasteless art and high maintenance marble. Selling the tower was his plan wasn't it; he didn't even tell you what he was doing did he?"

Before the widow Corrocco could nod again, Perkins jumped in by slapping the table hard and saying, "You're making my case for me, Firestone. If my client didn't know about the sale, how could it be her motive to hire a hit man."

"Your client didn't know about the sale, but you did and you told her because if the Tower sold there wouldn't be much need for a corporate lawyer would there?" Perkins leaned back looking flushed.

"Here's what I think; I think either one or both of you hired Bell to kill Martin and stop the sale, but the mass scale of the crime was not part of the deal. Madam Corrocco, your distress shows remorse; you didn't want this and you only deserve to pay for what you're guilty of, but I can't make that happen unless you tell me *everything*."

The room fell silent, so Firestone leaned in and reapplied the pressure, "To clarify, Mr. Perkins, you are no longer a lawyer. You were eligible for disbarment the minute I openly accused you of these crimes and you did not deny your involvement."

"You two are welcome to retain lawyers to represent you in this discussion but I already have clearance from the DA to have your charges of terrorism reduced to conspiracy to commit murder instead, but the reduction in charges depends on your cooperation. You're not going to get a better deal than this."

Elise broke under the pressure, "What do you want to know?"

"We want that deal in writing..." Perkins protested.

"You'll have it." Firestone growled, then he turned his attention back to Elise, "How did you get in touch with Bell?"

"I didn't," Elise answered, "The man I dealt with was much older and had an accent that seemed British to me..." As she continued to describe the man that she had dealt with, Firestone recognized who she was referring to. He kept thinking, *'there's no way, it cannot be him; can it?'*

Firestone snapped back to reality when he heard Elise Corrocco say, "I knew about him because Martin had mentioned him in passing a few times. Martin said he was a fixer; someone who makes problems go away."

Firestone pulled his phone from his pocket and brought a picture up on it. He showed the picture to Corrocco and Perkins asking, "Is this the man you dealt with?" They nodded and Firestone felt that the situation was now a different ball game because the man that they had identified was the same man who shot Leah Fong on her first mission with Firestone; he was the one who got away those ten years ago, Amilio Scarleto.

Chapter 15

Firestone ran out of the interview room without saying another word to his interviewees. He was so determined to get to Angelique's, he barely closed the door of the interrogation room behind him. His walk from the interrogation room to Angelique's cubical was a blur, "Angelique, I need you to activate the tracking device we planted in this cell phone."

Angelique immediately recognized the number Firestone had given her and struggled to accept that Firestone was employing a tactic that the agency was planning to save for a planned operation still two months away. "Are you sure Anthony? If you blow this, it *will* cost you your career and you could be brought up on criminal charges."

"I realize that," Firestone said. His tone was so sober that he barely recognized his own voice, "but the widow Corrocco and her lawyer Perkins confirmed that Amilio Scarleto has a connection to the bombing at the Carlton Tower."

It took Angelique a few seconds, but she eventually reluctantly activated the tracker. Within about ninety seconds, a satellite map of the world overtook her screens and refined to a map of the US, and then to their fair city. After a few more seconds of adjusting, the red dot representing the tracker's signal settled on a small, private airfield just outside the cities' limits.

Firestone patted Angelique's shoulder appreciatively then sped off towards the airfield.

Firestone's engine and brakes screeched simultaneously as he lurched to a stop just beyond the chain-link fencing that separated the runways from the parking space at the air field. Firestone awkwardly triple-parked and left the engine running with the hazard lights blinking.

He immediately recognized Scarleto's private plane from that ten-year-old mission in Africa. It had been washed and repainted, but the inexpensive surface repairs couldn't hide the obvious dents that still remained from Firestone's machine-gun fire. It was definitely Scarleto's plane and it was idling on the taxiway preparing to leave, again! The tracker also indicated Scarleto was on the plane and every nerve in Firestone's body was telling him that Bell and the nameless bomber were on it as well.

Backup was approaching fast, but not fast enough for Firestone. He would *not* lose Scarleto and his right-hand men again.

Firestone shook the fencing as he considered climbing it; the sound caused Bell to appear and stare in his direction on the staircase of the idling plane. "Don't bother

Gramps," A cocky Bell shouted across the tarmac through a megaphone. "Even if you could climb that fence, this plane and I will be speeding away before your feet hit the ground a second time." Bell gave a meaningless wave to Firestone as he turned and began to disappear up the plane's steps.

Firestone grit his teeth for a brief moment. As much as it pained him, he knew Bell was right; he wouldn't be able to apprehend Bell by the climbing the fence, but he quickly got another, more questionable, idea.

Firestone removed his gun from his belt and fed the barrel through a link in the fencing. He then fired a shot that landed squarely in Bell's back. Firestone saw Bell sprawl out and fall forward, then slump down to the bottom of the staircase. Ordinarily, a shooting like this would be questionable or even prosecutable, but Firestone no longer cared about anything but stopping these men.

With Bell sufficiently incapacitated, Firestone holstered his weapon and began climbing the fence. Firestone hoped that Bell's condition would be enough to stall the takeoff, but halfway up Firestone saw two men dressed as flight crew begin to pull Bell back up the steps into the plane and he realised that Scarleto had prepared his staff for something like this to happen. Things were moving too quickly for Firestone. "Hey, STOP! I'm a Federal Agent!" He shouted desperately as he climbed. He tried to give them pause, but the men ignored him blatantly.

Firestone released his grip on the fencing and dropped himself down on the other side and realign and shoot. Firestone emptied his gun towards the plane, knowing that there was too much tarmac for him to run across in time.

As he shot, he saw the invading men jump, bob, and weave. He recognized that he shot one of them twice and hit Bell twice more. Still they somehow managed to get themselves and Bell into the plane.

After that, Firestone felt as though he were having an out-of-body experience as he watched the door of the plane fold in. Then the large machine pulled away from the bloodied steps, taxied down the runway, and eventually took off.

Firestone stared hopelessly at the climbing plane as his reinforcements pulled in behind him loudly.

Chapter 16

A flushed and defeated Firestone sat slumped in a chair, facing the director's desk. Director Meyer was reading Firestone the riot act yet again; this time, he was rattling off all of Firestone's offences. "Firstly, you blow our secret weapon against Amilio Scarleto and opt to go crazed-cowboy and fight him yourself." Meyer Shouted. "Because of that, the plane was gone before the support team even arrived. *WHAT DO YOU HAVE TO SAY FOR YOURSELF?*"

Firestone was teary eyed, not because Meyer was getting to him, but because he was struggling to accept that Amilio Scarleto escaped again and had a very efficient bomber with him. Eventually he said, "Bell was on the same plane as the signal, it's possible Amilio could assume we followed Bell there and not his phone's signal. Our 'secret weapon' is likely still secure and Bell is dead..."

"Bell is a ringleader and Amilio can easily take his place as a ringleader. The person we needed to neutralize was the bomber and we didn't. Also you only saw Bell get shot by you three times; perhaps he's not dead, stranger things have happened. There is no good here Firestone."

Meyer exhaled furiously and said, "Fortunately, I have an opportunity for you to redeem yourself Firestone." Firestone looked up and Meyer continued, "Agent Leah Fong is officially seventy-two hours late to check in with her operational handler. No one can find her, so we're officially listing her as a missing person."

"Amilio's got her." A stricken Firestone stated.

"We don't know that for certain, but that's what we're thinking. I want you to investigate her disappearance."

"We're also assigning Detective Donna Sparks to work with you for fear that everyone in this office, yourself included, may be too close to this and she is a qualified and impartial investigator that you worked very well with…"

"Whatever just tell me everything I need to know to find Leah." A flustered Firestone begged.

"First we need to read you into her mission." Firestone nodded and listened eagerly.

"Leah was investigating allegations of human trafficking coming from the Chinese Triads. We planted her in the heart of the Asian community and when she last reported, she'd successfully become the girlfriend of one of the gang's leaders."

"The romance was part of the script. She was supposed to strain the relationship in the hopes that the annoyed boyfriend would place her in the trafficking program."

"We had the best tracking technology in the world on Leah, but it's all gone dark. She could still be trapped within the Triad organization, but apparently there's chatter on the streets that suggests otherwise..."

"Still, this file contains all of the details Leah gave us on the Triads and backstopped ID's for you and Sparks, should you feel the need to embed yourselves in the gang also."

Firestone snatched up the file and sped towards the door. Meyer called after him, "And Anthony,"

Firestone pivoted.

"Good luck."

Firestone felt he didn't need luck as he left his Director's office. He had a second chance and, this time, Scarleto would not escape.

TO BE CONTINUED...

READ: SECOND STRIKE

COMING SOON

Made in the USA
Middletown, DE
04 May 2017